T0209087

WHY MUST I CHASE DA CAT?

DARN OLDHAM

iUniverse

WHY MUST I CHASE DA CAT?

This is a work of fiction. All the characters, names, incidents, organizations, and dialogue in this novel are either the products of the author's imagination or are used fictitiously.

iUniverse books may be ordered through booksellers or by contacting:

iUniverse
1663 Liberty Drive
Bloomington, IN 47403
www.iuniverse.com
844-349-9409

Because of the dynamic nature of the Internet, any web addresses or links contained in this book may have changed since publication and may no longer be valid. The views expressed in this work are solely those of the author and do not necessarily reflect the views of the publisher, and the publisher hereby disclaims any responsibility for them.

Any people depicted in stock imagery provided by Getty Images are models, and such images are being used for illustrative purposes only. Certain stock imagery © Getty Images.

ISBN: 978-1-6632-1138-5 (sc)
ISBN: 978-1-6632-1139-2 (e)

Library of Congress Control Number: 2020923415

Print information available on the last page.

iUniverse rev. date: 01/21/2021

ACKNOWLEDGMENTS

At the top, I would like to thank the entity at the top, God. Thank you for giving me the wherewithal to be the me that I am, as imperfect as I am.

Also, I want to thank my family, the Oldhams, in Detroit, my sister, Annie Beard, my brothers, Kenny and Keith, my brother Gary and my Oldhams who art in Heaven, especially my mother, Ruth, my father, Paul, my brothers, Paul Jr. and Kevin. And thank all the other Oldhams, my nieces, nephews, and cousins in Detroit, California, and other parts of the country. Facebook put me in touch with a whole lot of you and the Lumbards (on my mother's side) and I am *very* happy about that.

Thanks to my Los Angeles family, which includes the Amigos— Don Derbigny, Dave Edwards, Arnold Turner, Stanley Stain, Ray Charles Jr.,—and the four Amigos in heaven—Jonathan Holloway, Robert Betts, Roland Wirt, and Spaulding Settle. It also includes the Pinochle Crew: Larry Phillips, Doc Darry Jacobs, Thris Van Taylor, and Gil Teel. You ALL make Los Angeles home to me and my beautiful wife, Barbara.

I also want to thank the authors who influenced me the most, who made me want to write in the first-person vernacular, Richard S. Prather and Max Shulman. I couldn't put their novels down as a teenager and while in Vietnam.

And lastly, I want to thank my wife, Barbara Moore Oldham, who made me the happiest man in the world on October 20, 2018. Your spirit, positive attitude and love keeps me grounded. I love you, Baby.

CONQUESTS

BOOTY'S ONLY SKIN DEEP

SOMETIMES, WHEN HE'S *REAL* HORNY, A GUY DOESN'T GIVE A HECK what a woman looks like, just as long as she's willing to give it up.

Me? I'm not like that. I don't care how horny I am; I'm *always* going to care how the chick looks. I'm very particular about who I introduce to "Junior."

Now, I ain't gonna front; I have acquainted Junior to a few ladies who were not at least a seven in the face, but each time, her body was a ten. Something on her *had* to be a ten—if not her face, then her rack.

But I would never take them out in public.

No one has ever seen me on a date with a babe that was not a seven or above. And that has been hard to do. Even booty calls wanted to be wined and dined. Take the Bertha incident, for instance.

Bertha was built as if I had planned her myself. Like the fictional Dobie Gillis said, she had "no unsightly bulges, but several sightly ones." She was five feet seven; had a nice, slender neck that came down to soft shoulders with tapered arms; and her breasts were perfect pears, about 36D. She had a small waist that swelled out to thirty-eight-inch hips that swept around to form a booty to beat all booties.

It looked plump yet firm. I knew that squeezing it would be like squeezing a sponge. It would give in and then just spring right back out with all its juiciness. Her long legs were very shapely, and if I looked closely, I could see fine, sandy hairs on them. I used to have a thing about females with fine hair on their legs. That was a turn-on to me.

However, above that slender neck was a face that would make even the Terminator hesitate. I mean she wasn't ugly, now. To me no one is ugly. *Ugly* is not a term that I use to describe someone's looks. I use it to represent one's personality but not one's appearance. So let's just say she was *lacking* when it came to good looks.

She was very plain and homely. Celie from *The Color Purple* would've looked like Miss America next to her. Wearing makeup was against her principles, I guessed. That was cool, because I don't think makeup would have helped her pockmarked face much anyway. She had very bushy eyebrows and a trace of a mustache—hairy legs sometimes come with an abundance of hair in other areas—and she wore glasses and a wig.

Women with glasses were a turn-on for me too. Women who wore wigs were not, especially if it was one of those Zodys department store wigs.

I met her at one of our house parties at our crib, the Mini-Mansion. I was circulating with one of my roommates, Doc, greeting folks and checking out the new female attendees.

We made our way into the solarium, and I saw this figure down at the other entrance talking to some other female figures. They all had nice figures, but the one with her back to me was in a form-fitting pink dress that hugged her body like pink skin.

"*Got*-dayum!" I exclaimed in admiration of the sleek form with the small waist, moderately wide hips, and the imprints of a helluva booty.

"You don't want that-ski," Doc cautioned.

"And why not?" I asked. That's when she turned around to say something to one of her friends. "Got-*dayum*!" I said with disgust as I saw her face.

"*That's* why not." Doc smiled. "Now, I know you're a booty man, but you're a face man too."

"Who told you." That wasn't a question. It was my way of being sarcastic—the same as saying "Duh" or "You got that right" or "Obviously" or "Very perceptive, dummy."

Doc and I continued through the solarium past her group and then separated as we scouted the ladies to see whom we would be inviting to stay when the party started winding down.

There was a long line waiting for the restroom downstairs, I noticed, as I was heading from the kitchen through the dining room to the library. I felt a hand on my shoulder.

"Excuse me," a sweet feminine voice said.

I turned around to face the speaker. It was the sexy body in the pink dress.

I smiled. And it was hard to smile at that face. "Can I help you?"

"Could you please tell me if there is another bathroom available?"

I hesitated for a moment before I said, "Uh, yes, come with me." I led her up the stairs to one of the other bathrooms. I tried the doorknob, but it was locked. "There's someone in there, but they shouldn't be long." I turned to go back downstairs.

She stopped me. "You're one of the hosts, right?"

"Yes," I said in a friendly tone. I noticed that she had pretty eyes behind those slightly thick glasses. And her firm nipples were pressing against the fabric of that pink dress. *She doesn't have a bra on!* I thought.

"Let me stop being rude and introduce myself. I'm Bertha."

"I'm Davey," I replied. "Are you having a good time?"

"Definitely. Quite frankly, I knew I would. My uncle's residence is around the corner on Presidio; he shared with us the fact that you guys give nice gatherings."

"Us?"

"Oh, I'm accompanied by my two cousins. I'm dwelling with them and my uncle for a while. This surely is a 'pretty-people party.'"

Except for you, I thought. But, of course, I didn't say that. There was something fascinating about her though, besides her body. I could tell she was a very sharp young lady just by her conversation and the look in her eyes. And that was another turn-on for me.

The bathroom door opened, and Sheila, a friend of ours, came out.

"Davey, it's running low on paper in there," she informed me.

"I'll get some more," I said, heading toward the upper storage closet.

"I'll wait," Bertha offered.

"No, no, you're good, girl," Sheila told her. "It's not *that* low." Bertha went on in and closed the door.

I grabbed a couple of rolls from the closet and returned to the bathroom door.

"Is that your new stuff?" Sheila asked with a disapproving look.

"Naw, naw," I replied, knowing she knew better. "I'm just being friendly."

"I was gittin' ready to say." Sheila laughed. "I know you can do better than that tonight. *Much* better."

"Who told you."

She went back downstairs chuckling.

The bathroom door opened.

"Thank you very much, Davey," Bertha said as she came out.

"You're welcome very much."

"I tell my students that it's mind over matter and that they can sustain as long as they need to, but I think the two glasses of wine made matter override my mind."

"Your students?" I pried as I quickly dashed into the restroom and placed the two rolls on the counter before returning to the hallway.

"Yes, I do some training at an arts center in Hollywood."

"I should've known."

"How so?"

"Your demeanor, the way you talk."

"Is that good or bad?"

"It's not bad," I assured. "But I've never seen a teacher with a body like yours." I was always more direct with ladies that were not that attractive. It's like I didn't care if I turned them off or on. I guess it was because I really wasn't hitting on them, but just flirting with them as a favor to *them*, for *their* benefit.

"I'll take that as a compliment."

With that face, she probably doesn't get many, I figured.

"It was," said I.

"Thank you. Well, let me go and locate my cousins." She turned and headed toward the stairs. I stood there and watched her sexy walk; her butt cheeks shifted and jiggled with each step. *Yo' turn, my turn, yo' turn, my turn …* I felt myself getting aroused.

"Uh, wait, Bertha," I called out as she took one step down. She stopped. "Why don't you give me your number so I can invite you and your cousins to the club we run also?"

She smiled. "I would like that." She didn't look all that bad when she smiled, but still bad. She had a wide mouth with nice, full lipstickless lips. The mustache ruined the picture.

"Let me get a pen and some paper." I went into my bedroom to get a pen and pad off my nightstand. When I looked up, she was standing in my doorway.

"Nice room," she complimented, looking at my king-sized bed covered with a black plush comforter, held together by my black-and-walnut Ashley Furniture headboard and footboard. She glanced at my thirty-two-inch Sony sitting on the black TV console in front of the bed, the black leather love seat, the black oak twin nightstand, the chest of drawers and dresser set, the Bose stereo system in the corner, and the door leading out to the balcony.

"Thank you," I said, moving toward her with the pen and pad. "Here, write down your info."

She accepted them and wrote her name and number down. I was looking at those nipple imprints as I walked behind her to push the bedroom door closed. I didn't want anyone to see her with me. I had a reputation to uphold.

My eyes roamed her entire sensuous body as I stood there behind her. She turned to hand me the pen and pad. I took her hand and pulled her to me as I backed against the door. I put an arm around her small waist, drawing her body up against mine. She just looked at me without saying a word. My eyes closed; I just wanted to handle that body, not look at that face. Lifting her chin with a finger, I kissed her lips softly and then backed off and looked into her eyes. She seemed to be saying, "Do what you want to," without saying a word.

I lowered my head to kiss her again and felt her arms go around my neck as I kissed her harder, this time with my hands on her butt, squeezing the plump muscle as she pressed closer. She whimpered.

After a very long kiss with me massaging her buttocks, we broke apart. I gently pulled her toward the bed. She balked nervously.

"Uh, I … I got to, uh … I have to go find my cousins," she said.

I wasn't going to press it, even though I felt that she would've given in. The party was still young, and there were plenty of fresh, friendly, *pretty* fish floating around downstairs, waiting to be hit on.

"Okay." I went to the door to open it, making sure no one was in the hallway or coming up the stairs.

"Give me your number also," Bertha requested. I did so quickly so she could head back downstairs before anyone saw us together.

I gave her a couple of minutes before I headed back down.

Dab, my other roommate, was coming up the stairs with a couple of cuties.

"I heard you was up here with an ug-mo," he informed me.

Sheila's big mouth, I deducted.

"Man, why don't you be cool with that kind of talk," I reprimanded, indicating the two with him. For all we knew they could be Bertha's cousins, and I didn't want to hurt her feelings if the "ug-mo" comment got back to her. *Besides, she wasn't that ugly,* I thought, *just plain. Plainly not good-looking, but plain enough for me not to want to be seen with her.* But I still was considerate of her feelings.

"Davey, no one cares who you're with," Dab commented.

"Yeah, well then why did you bring it up?" I asked. I was concerned about Bertha's feelings, even though I knew I wasn't going to be asking her out or anything. However, her sexuality did turn me on somewhat.

"Uh, ladies, go 'head. The restroom is right down there." Dab pointed the two ladies in the direction of the toilet. After they left us, he turned to me. "What's up with your memory?"

"What?"

"Remember the contest?" he reminded.

"What con—oh shit!" It came back to me. At the beginning of the month, Dab was ragging on Doc about his lack of cutie-pie dates. We were at the Stinking Rose, a garlic restaurant on LaCienega's Restaurant Row that we favored on Thursdays for happy hour.

Doc had gotten a little perturbed at the ribbing he was getting from us. That's when he proposed a contest. For the next two months, whoever was seen out with the worse-looking babe would have to buy groceries and booze for the whole household for two months.

"I forgot all about that," I admitted.

"Yeah, well, we got a few weeks left," Dab said after making a quick calculation. "A word to the wise—"

"Is sufficient," I told him. "I'll be keeping tabs on you guys' dates for the next three weeks for sure, especially Doc. Thanks for the heads up."

"You know how we do. One dawg to another." We tapped fists, and he headed to the restroom door and knocked three times. I saw the end of a red towel that he had stuffed in his back pocket. I knew that meant he was planning on using the laundry room soon.

The laundry room was behind the house, attached to the garage. We used the red towel to let each other know that we were "knocking off a chunk" back there during a party. We displayed it in the window or left part of it sticking out of the door.

The party was getting more crowded now. Folks were sitting on the stairs, and more were coming up to use the restroom and staying upstairs. I leaned on the banister, contemplating the contest as I looked down at the ocean of folks enjoying themselves. I went back downstairs to wade in it.

It was "Cutie-pie City-ski," as Doc was prone to say.

Now, Doc wasn't a bad-looking brother. He was the same height as I, six four, but weighed about ten to fifteen pounds more than my two-oh-five. He had curly hair and a neatly trimmed mustache, which gave him a sophisticated Billy Dee Williams look, and he wore glasses. Plus he was a dentist. Doctor Joseph Holliday—Doc Holliday, we all called him. He had the habit of adding *ski* at the end of some nouns. It started after *brewski* became a popular term for beer.

The house—the Mini-Mansion—was his. He grew up in it. It had that name because of its size, contour, and the two large white columns that framed the front porch of the two-story, red-brick structure, giving it a plantation motif. In addition, it was one of the few houses in the View Park area that had an adjoining lot next to it that was big enough to build another house on.

Joseph's father had purchased both lots back in the '50s when he opened his law firm. He had originally planned to extend the house onto both properties but never got around to it. Then, as his firm prospered, he and Joseph's mother decided to move into Bel-Air, where some of his celebrity clients lived. They gave the house to their only son.

It was a fun house, what with the pool table in the den, the swimming pool, the Jacuzzi, and the gazebo in the backyard. Also, they had fruit trees on both lots: avocado, lemon, orange, and apple.

The neighborhood was called View Park. It was created in the early 1930s as the Olympic village for the '32 Games. It was on high ground, hence the name. As a matter of fact, some of the streets in the area were named after streets in Greece, the home of the Olympics. The street we lived on, Olympiad Drive, had been the main thoroughfare in the village back then.

With the house and all, Doc had all the tools to catch the women, but his taste in women was suspect. We didn't know what the reason was. Did he lack confidence? He told us about growing up as a chubby little Poindexter-type kid that got picked on and the girls not liking him. Was self-doubt still instilled in him? It was a rare occasion to see him with a chick that Dab or I would think twice about being with.

Now Dab and I bumped heads over the same lady sometimes. I was living in an apartment in the Mid-Wilshire area and Dab was living in a condo in Fox Hills when Doc took over the house. He asked us to move in and take our time finding houses of our own. We readily agreed.

Daniel Dabineau, known as Dab to his friends, was a partner in a men's apparel business. His apparel company, Street Smart, was a new urban wear manufacturer that was slowly catching on in LA. He and his partner were planning to go nationwide with it.

His culinary skills were legendary in our circle. He was shorter than Doc and me, about five feet ten. Sometimes I saw a Napoleon complex in him. He *had* to be better at everything. He was darker too. I figured that was why he was mostly attracted to light-skinned sisters and White women. Dab was also very charming with the women and used that and his cooking *and* his generous spending habit to weave a web that most of them couldn't resist.

Me? I'm Davey Stein. I'm part owner of an employment agency over in the Mid-Wilshire area, the Stein and Frank Agency. I'm sure you can see why my name came *first*. My office was in the same high-rise building that housed Doc's dentist office. That's how we met.

There were quite a few of my ex-girlfriends at the party, which was all right with me; that's why I invited them. I always felt that if we were friends before we dated, we could remain friends after the lust was gone. Sometimes, however, the lust wasn't gone. In those cases, we left the door open for some late-night creeping.

"Hey you," a feminine voice said behind me as I was talking to some friends in the kitchen.

I turned to see Evelyn, a girl I used to go out with. She was looking delectable in a brown-and-cream flowery blouse and brown skirt ensemble that showed off her supple figure.

"Hey you back at ya," I said.

"Nice party, as usual."

"Glad you could make it."

"Didn't really think it would matter with all the women you guys got here."

"Good-looking ladies always matter." I leaned closer to her ear. "Especially if they look good and taste good too."

Evelyn smiled. "Well, you know I like helping you with your appetite."

"Can you help me tonight?" I laughed.

"Try me," she said coyly, swishing her butt emphatically as she walked away.

A little later, Renee, another ex, sidled up to me dressed in a form-fitting black outfit.

"You'd better stop looking so good," I warned her.

"I can't help it."

"Who're you here with?"

"Susan, but we came in separate cars. Hint, hint."

"Well, see me before you leave," I requested. "Hint, hint."

We both laughed.

I went into the cleared-out living room and saw a beauty I had dated named Honore dancing with Borneo "Born" Luckey, a private investigator whose office was in the same building that my employment agency and Doc's dentist office was in. She looked in my direction and winked. I winked back. I saw Saturday Knight dancing with Denn Elliot, one of my old college buddies. She avoided my eyes. Melody was rocking with her new beau in the corner. She waved at me. Sheila and her boyfriend, Cornell, were swinging next to Vanessa and Venita. They were gyrating in the middle of the floor with Richard Butts and Sterling Sutton, two of our partners from our Friday nightclub, Rendezvous. Vanessa noticed me and blew me a kiss; I guessed Fashion Fair was on hiatus. The dance floor was crowded.

Good-looking ladies made a so-so party a great party. I think even the ladies felt better about being at a party when they could look around and see other good-looking ladies there. It made them feel as if they were in the right place—as though it would've been a travesty not to be there. They were there just to represent. I know the guys appreciated it. That's why the men knew better than to miss a party at the Mini-Mansion. There was always plenty of food, booze, and good-looking women.

Throughout the evening, I noticed Bertha and her cousins

enjoying themselves. I saw quite a few guys giving Bertha's body the once-over more than once.

A few times, as I passed through a room that they were in, Bertha would look up and give me a smile. Each time, I felt myself getting aroused. *What the hell is that about?* I wondered.

I knew the answer. It was about that body—that luscious booty.

The party was thinning out, which is always a good time to start making reservations. That's when you make plans to take someone to breakfast or have her stay to *be* breakfast.

"I hid my purse in your bedroom," Renee informed me as I was standing in the front doorway, watching two guys walk Bertha and her two good-looking cousins to their car. "I'm going to go get it and wait up there for you."

"That'll be nice," I said.

She pinched my butt and went up the stairs.

"I see you don't need me tonight," Evelyn said, walking up and eyeing Renee going up the stairs.

"Naw, naw, naw," I said, "she just going to get her purse."

"Good, then we should have breakfast tomorrow morning," she suggested. "Should I call you or *nudge* you?"

I chuckled. I had used that same line on her when we first met months ago.

"Uh-ruh ..." I began.

"'Uh-ruh' nothing. Should I hang around or not?" asked Evelyn.

"No, I, uh ... I had one, uh ... one drink too many," I lied. "I'm going to, uh, pass out as soon as my head hits the pillow. Plus we've been working hard on this party all day. I'm just beat."

She gave in. "Yeah, uh-huh, okay. I'll talk to you later."

I think she knew the truth. She was cool like that, though, which I counted on. Sometimes you count on a woman to help you lie to her. They do it for their own self-esteem, I think. They don't want to catch you lying to them when the truth might hurt their feelings, so they go along with the lie that you're weaving. It makes them feel better—makes them feel like, "Hey, Bub, you're not getting over on me. I know better. I'm just letting you slide."

I slid on up to my bedroom. Renee was in the bathroom. The telephone rang. I picked up on the first ring.

"I can't stop thinking about you," the feminine voice said.

I smiled. "Who is this?"

"It's Bertha," she answered. "Can you come around the corner?"

Without hesitation, I agreed. "Oh, *hell* yeah!"

She gave me directions. I hung up as a naked Renee came out of the bathroom.

"I have to make a quick run," I told her, picking up my car keys off the dresser. "I'll be right back."

"Don't take too long."

Why am I doing this? I chided myself as I drove up the hill on Olympiad one block to Presidio, made a right, crossed Mt. Vernon, and looked for her address on the left. *I have a pretty, sexy, horny lady waiting in my bed, and here I am going to see a mud duck. A mud duck with one of the most incredible bodies that I've ever seen, albeit, but a mud duck nonetheless. Or is it just about new stuff?*

As I parked my car and walked around the side of the main house to the guesthouse in the back, as she had instructed me, I kept reminding myself of the reasons why I shouldn't be seeing this girl. *She wears a wig, I told myself, and I hate wigs. Her complexion is shot. She is a three at most, out of a scale of one to ten. She wears thick glasses that make her eyes look bigger than they are, making her look like a frog peeking through ice. She has very bushy eyebrows, a mustache,* and yet …

I rang her doorbell. Celie—I mean, Bertha—must have been standing there waiting for me, because she opened the door immediately and pulled me inside.

Folks, I'm not going to go into details. Suffice it to say that it was two hours of the most awesome sex I'd ever experienced. The woman was an animal. It was as though she had been in jail and hadn't had sex for years. Or she was a nymphomaniac. I didn't know which.

As we lay there talking afterward, I found out that she was a Sagittarian, and then I understood. I had read a book a while back called *Sexual Astrology*. It stated that when a Sagittarian woman and an Aquarian man get together in a bedroom, they should charge admission to show others what should be done in a bedroom. And, yes, I'm an Aquarian. An audience would have gotten their money's worth that night, especially with the two encores. And I had held back somewhat. Remember: I had a "bucket-naked" girl waiting for me at home that I had to attend to as well.

"I, uh … I gotta go," I said when I felt Bertha's hand stroking me, getting me ready for round four.

"Are you sure?" she asked as her wigged head slid under the covers.

Yep, she still had that wig on *and* her thick glasses. I wondered what her real hair, if she had any, must look like if she was so afraid to take the damn wig off even at bedtime.

She had gone to the bathroom a couple of times during our rendezvous. I figured she was still reacting to the wine she'd had at the party or she had to fix the wig.

"Yeah, yeah, the fellas are going to be pissed at me already 'cause, uh, we're supposed to be, uh, cleaning up right now."

"Okay," she yawned. "Can you let yourself out?" I had wrung out all her energy.

I was smiling the smile of a job well done as I drove back around the corner to the house.

When I crept into my bedroom, Renee was sound asleep with the TV on. I turned it off and slipped under the covers. She didn't move.

⟿

"Why didn't you wake me when you got in last night?" Renee asked, climbing on top of me a few hours later. "What time did you get back?"

"Oh, I was, uh, only gone fifteen, twenty minutes. You were knocked out."

"Well, I'm not knocked out now."

And we went at it. She slid down my body to speak into the mike, and I turned her around to talk to the Y. It was a very interesting conversation. Sixty-nine was a great year. We decided to introduce the Y to the mike. They got along famously. Junior was a hit, as usual.

Renee had a nice body and was pretty, and of course, she had a nice derriere. Any woman I got involved with had to have a nice butt. But I found myself lying there next to her thinking of Bertha's booty.

She had a pretty booty. It had her pecan shell color, was perfectly shaped, and was plump, not flabby—firm enough to hold its shape even when she was lying on her stomach. I thought about the old Temptations song "Beauty's Only Skin Deep." The question was, Who looks beneath the skin? I guess I was doing it this time. Or was I only seeing the skin—the pecan skin that covered Bertha's pretty booty?

Too bad I won't be seeing it anymore ... unless I get super horny again, I decided. *Bertha is a one-night stand.*

Two nights later, I was in her bed again.

Just like my first time there, she made a couple of trips to the bathroom. During her second trip, I fell asleep. *It must have taken her longer to get her wig back together,* I surmised as she shook me awake. She always looked more refreshed when she returned to the bed.

Before we went at it again, she invited me to meet her for happy hour the next day. I didn't want to be seen in public with her by anyone that I knew. That little guesthouse was our private world, and I didn't want to venture out of it with her.

I mean, Bertha had an inner beauty—and an outer booty—that was fascinating, but being seen with her might cause a situation that could hurt her feelings. Plus I had a contest I didn't want to lose. *I am doing this for her good,* I lied to myself. I told her I had an appointment.

Okay, I reflected as I was leaving late that night, *it must be the Sagittarian thing, but no more of this. I've got cutie-pies to see.*

Three days later, I was hitting it again. She wanted to take me to dinner the next day. Her treat. I told her that I was on a strict liquid diet.

This has got to stop, I thought. *I don't want her to think that she was just a booty call.*

Her booty called me the next day to say that she had some tickets to go to a screening of the new Denzel movie that evening. I told her that I had something to do.

Almost a week went by before I hooked up with her again.

"Davey, my cousin is having a grand opening party at her salon tomorrow," she said as we were lying in her bed after sex. "Wanna go?" She straightened her wig, which had gone awry as usual during our strenuous sexual bout.

"Uh-ruh ... tomorrow, huh?" I said, trying to come up with another excuse.

"Yes, well, the next day, Friday, is the official grand opening, but we're having the party tomorrow. I'll get there about five. You can come by any time after that. It'll probably go till ten o'clock or so."

Oh, so I won't have to come with her, I thought. *I can show up as another attendee and make it appear as though we just have a casual relationship—that we're not together, not a couple. That'll work.*

"Okay, I'll come," I said as I kissed her on the forehead. *This way I can dispel any thoughts that she might have about me not wanting to be seen with her too.*

⌒

It was about six thirty when I arrived at the salon over on Manchester the next day. It was fairly crowded with about a hundred people. Her cousin had a table set up with hors d'oeuvres against one wall and a bar against another wall. Also, there was a trio playing some jazz. I was surprised to see Doc and Dab there.

"How did you guys hear about this?" I asked Dab. He was in the food line, while Doc was getting a drink on the other side of the room.

"Cheryl invited us," he said matter-of-factly.

"Cheryl?" I quizzed.

"Uh, yeah, Cheryl—the woman who owns the shop," he shared. "The one who's giving this shindig. She was at our last party with her sister and that girl." He pointed to Bertha, who was chatting with some folks at a table. "How did *you* hear about it?"

"Uh, that girl," I said, indicating Bertha.

He smiled. "Oh, okay."

"Hey, Davey-ski," Doc greeted, walking up with a cognac in hand. "Who told you about this?"

"Uh, Bertha called me," I lied. Actually, she had rolled over in bed to tell me.

"Oh, the *brick house* who looks like an *outhouse*." Doc laughed.

"That's cold, man," I said disapprovingly.

Just then, Bertha looked up and saw me and waved. It seemed like *everyone* in there turned around to see who she was waving at. I gave her a quick halfhearted wave. Dab and Doc looked at me too.

"You ain't, uh … you ain't hitting that, are you?" Dab asked.

"Give me a break, man," I scoffed as I headed to the bar to get my signature drink, a cuba libre with Myers's rum. *Maybe it was a bad idea to come here*, I thought. The fellas followed me to the bar.

"Hey, man, if you're hitting it, that's your business," Doc said with a smile.

"Who told you," I said. "But I'm *not*. Okay?"

"Hi, honey," Bertha greeted, walking between the guys and kissing me on the cheek.

Dab and Doc looked at me with smirks on their faces.

"Looks like someone is going to be buying groceries for two months-ski," Doc said to Dab.

"Yep, I think we have a winner," Dab agreed.

"Fuck it," I said. I grabbed Bertha, closed my eyes, and kissed her passionately on the lips.

Dab, Doc, *and* Bertha looked at me with wide-eyed surprise.

Her cousin Cheryl was on the microphone. "Folks, I want to thank you all for coming tonight. This is the culmination of months of planning by my sister, my cousin, and me. Donna, Bertha, join me up here, please."

"I'll be right back," Bertha said, excusing herself. She joined her cousins up on the makeshift platform where the jazz trio had been performing.

"As some of you know," Cheryl continued, "my sister, Donna, is the hairstylist for some of the popular sitcoms you see on TV, and my cousin, Bertha, works as a top special effects and makeup artist for the studios."

"What?" I said. Doc and Dab just grinned.

"They're both partners here," Cheryl went on. "Donna will be doing hair, and Bertha will do makeup, by appointments only. Keep in mind they're both very busy people, but we have stylists and makeup folks trained by them."

"Huh? What did she say?" I asked.

"Now let me show you some of their work. Bertha, please reveal!"

Bertha walked to the front of the platform and dramatically pulled off her wig. Underneath she had her real hair bundled inside a hair net. She removed the net to reveal sandy-colored curly hair with golden highlights that hung down to her shoulders.

I stood in front of the bar with the fellas with my mouth agape.

"This style and the tint are the works of Donna," Cheryl announced. "Now let's see Bertha's work. Bertha, continue, please."

Bertha's hands went to her face, and she peeled. The layers of pockmarked skin on both sides of her face came off to reveal smooth, pecan-colored skin. Her hands then removed the thin layer of a mustache and the bushy eyebrows. She took off the thick glasses and flung them to the back of the platform. Still facing us, she was handed a damp cloth and a compact. Bertha wiped her face, applied a little foundation and lip gloss, and delicately lined her eyes. Then she shook her head to loosen her hair and stood there with her hands on her hips, smiling and looking like Miss America—looking fantastic. The crowd reacted with applause, including several shouts of "You go, girl!" and shrill whistles.

I was dumbfounded.

"Folks, Bertha went around looking like that with all that goop on her face for two weeks, when originally it was only supposed to be for the last couple of days," Cheryl said, "but her cousin on her mother's side, Doctor Joseph Holliday over there, asked her to wear the makeup to his party to play a joke on someone."

I looked at Doc. "You motherfucka you!" I laughed.

He and Dab high-fived.

Yep, I went on and bought the groceries and booze—especially champagne—for the house for two whole months, with a smile on my face. And beautiful, booty-ful, sexy, freaky, creative Bertha and her two cousins came by often to help us partake of them.

PARTY'S OVER HERE

WHEN I FIRST OPENED MY EMPLOYMENT AGENCY WITH MY MARRIED business partner, George Frank, and before I moved into the Mini-Mansion with Dab and Doc, I lived in another part of LA. The area was simply called the Mid-Wilshire Area.

Wilshire Boulevard is probably the third-best-known street in Los Angeles, right after Sunset and Hollywood Boulevards. It runs east–west from downtown LA all the way to the Pacific Ocean in Santa Monica. The famous restaurant the Brown Derby was just a few blocks up the street there in Mid-Wilshire, right across the street from the Coconut Grove, which was in the Ambassador Hotel, where Robert Kennedy was assassinated.

Also in the Mid-Wilshire Area, north of the boulevard, were situated a cluster of apartment structures covering four parallel streets—Harvard, Hobart, Kingsley, and Ardmore—between Sixth Street and Third Street. Some of the finest angels in the City of Angels lived within that area. I'm talking flight attendants, models, actresses, singers, businesswomen, and college students, and it was alleged that some "working girls" who could entertain a guy in other ways called the area home too … but now, uh, you didn't hear that from me.

They were big, beautiful apartment complexes, well kept, with palm trees, swimming pools, Jacuzzis, steam rooms, game rooms, underground parking, and security gates. I mean, what respectable apartment complex in Los Angeles didn't have those amenities? Even the complexes in the Jungle had those enhancements back in the day.

Now, as I said, I had just started my employment agency business with my ex-army buddy and hadn't yet met the guys who, with me, would become known as the 3Ds.

In fact, I had just moved back to LA a few years earlier, after a stint in the army and going to college in DC and then spending some years in Atlanta.

Although I had a car, I decided that I wanted to live close enough to walk to work. I hated traffic of any kind, but rush-hour traffic I disliked the most.

Our office was on the sixteenth floor of the Travelers Insurance Building, which was at 3600 Wilshire Boulevard between Hobart and Kingsley, just three blocks from 444 S. Kingsley Dr., the building I decided to call home.

Walking to work was a treat, because I liked keeping in shape. And not only did I walk to work, but after I got there, I took the stairs, instead of the elevator, each morning to our suite. Yep, sixteen floors.

Now, I must admit, when I first started doing that, my legs were pretty pissed at me, and I would be sweating like a slave when I finally emerged on my floor. But gradually my body got used to it, and once all the sweating stopped, our staff became happier too.

But the exercise wasn't the only thing that made my walk to work a treat. The treat was seeing the mixture of females driving by, strolling by, getting dropped off, getting off buses, waiting for buses, and coming out of the restaurant on the corner or the Red Onion across the street, and seeing those who lived in the area walking to work, as I did.

The sight of a beautiful woman does things to me I can't explain. They revitalize me somehow, making my pulse race and my pupils dilate. They make me want to stay young forever, exercise more, look my best, smell my best, and be all that I can be. Or is that the army?

Anyway, I'd been living in the building for about a month now, and yet I still seemed to see a different COD every day. COD stands for "cutie on duty," which means that a lady is representing for *all* the foxes in the world.

When I moved in, the manager informed me that there were 180 units in the building, with six vacancies. He said that since he had a lot of applications for those vacancies, he was going to be very particular. I hoped that meant he was going to be choosing CODs. I mean, that's what I would've done if I were in his shoes. But since he was obviously gay, I think he was concerned more about a credit score between six hundred and eight hundred rather than whether they were tens or not.

Anyway, I lucked up and got the last one-bedroom unit in the front section of the three-story complex on the first floor. That meant I had a view of everyone coming and going through the front security gate, visiting the office, lounging in the lounge, playing in the game room, or utilizing the swimming pool and Jacuzzi, which were right outside my unit. So if I saw a honey that I liked, I could be on her like black on coal. Oh, I knew that it was going to be fun living there.

My male friends had been on me to throw a party and invite the ladies in the building so they could meet them. And I was contemplating it, but I really didn't make up my mind until *she* walked through that front gate.

I had just gotten in from the office and was into my regular routine. My stereo was tuned to the jazz station, and I was settled down on the couch, still in my suit, getting ready to go through my mail with a Miller Genuine Draft in hand.

I heard the clang of the front gate and looked up just in time to see this tall, long-haired, brown-skinned beauty fast-stepping past the pool and the office on into the lobby. Jumping up and almost spilling my brewski, I went to the patio door to get a better view. She was something else—very sexily built. Although she had on a loose-fitting dress, I could see the bouncing below her waist under that dress, which indicated a caboose that wasn't playing. When you added long, shapely legs; curved hips; and breasts that were perfectly pert to the package, you had a woman with potential. I saw all that with that quick glance.

I watched as she walked rapidly through the lobby and down the hall toward the mailboxes. Seeing this, I ran into the bedroom, where I had good view of the game room and the mailboxes, which were right outside of said room. That is, I could see the mailboxes *if* the double doors in the game room that led to the hallway were wide open, as they usually were. They were closed this time. *Damn!*

I shrugged and went back into the living room, noting the time. Five thirty.

And there she was again, briskly walking back through the lobby toward the elevators. *Okay, that means she doesn't stay on the first floor,* I deduced. I watched her as she pushed the call button for the elevator, looked through her mail nonchalantly, stepped back to let some folks exit the hoist, and then was lost from view as the doors closed. *Man, she was the best one I've seen in the building,* I told myself.

The next day, I was waiting at my bedroom window overlooking the swimming pool with my mail and beer when she came walking through the gate again. She had on a white pantsuit outfit, which outlined her posterior nicely. Yep, she had a great commode choker on her!

As she entered the complex, I switched over to the patio door to watch her at the mailboxes. I had made sure that the double doors in the game room were open when I retrieved my mail. I almost lost it as I watched her bend over to get to her box. She then went to the elevator and was gone. Her routine was the same the following day.

I decided that it was time for me to get down to business on the fourth day. For three days now, I had done nothing but observe her. I mean, you would think that I'd never seen a pretty girl before. But that wasn't it. I *have* seen pretty girls—plenty of them. And they *all* made me act as if I were obsessed.

To me, as with most men, a beautiful woman was an aphrodisiac. Looking at them and possibly interacting with them gets our blood boiling and gets us fantasizing about being with her—in every way.

And so it was with this lady—and had been for three days now. Today I was determined to meet her.

When I got in from work, I went straight to my bedroom window—no stopping at the mailbox, no Miller Genuine Draft. I wanted to be able to move out as soon as I saw her. I checked my watch. *She's usually here by now,* I told myself. To calm my nerves, I went to the fridge to grab a brewski anyway. As I was twisting the top off, I heard the clang of the gate.

There she was!

Without thinking, I set the beer on the counter, grabbed a pen, slid the patio door open, stepped back in, took a quick look at myself in the mirror, slipped out the patio door, and closed it behind me. It took four strides to cross the patio and enter the game room.

There were two guys shooting pool at one of the two tables in the room. We exchanged greetings as I went to the rack and selected a cue stick. I kept glancing toward the mailbox area while I casually walked around the other table, retrieved the balls from the pockets, and scattered them on the table.

"Yeah, she's a built motherfucka, all right," the shorter of the two guys commented to his companion as they progressed through their game.

"Anybody hitting on her?" the other guy asked.

"Shit, I don't know!" the shorter one replied. "But as soon as I get a chance, watch out!"

"Hey, I thought you said she was coming to the mailbox," the companion reminded Shorty.

"I thought she *was!*" Shorty shot back.

I thought so too, I thought, realizing that they were talking about Miss Fast-Stepper. I hurriedly left the room and headed for the elevator and watched the floor indicators above it. It stopped at the second floor and remained there.

On returning to the game room, I put the cue back in the rack and then went to the mailbox to check my mail. The guys were still shooting pool, but I felt them looking at me as I reached into my pants pocket for my keys, reached into the other pocket, and then went through my suit jacket pockets before realizing that in my haste to get in position to talk to the girl, I had left my keys in the apartment.

"Uh, anything wrong, man?" Shorty inquired with a smile.

"Naw," I lied as I headed out onto the patio to my patio door.

I pulled at the door to open it, but it wouldn't slide. *Okay, it just need a little more elbow grease.* I tried to slide it again, a little harder. The thing wouldn't move. *Okay, let me stop playing with this thing,* I told myself, and I really put some muscle into it. Still no good. That's when I realized that I had locked myself out. I looked around, and the two pool shooters were getting a kick out of my predicament.

With my head held high, I went to the office and got the assistant manager to unlock my door for me—after she got her chuckle on too.

The next day, after work, I was at my post by the bedroom window again—with my keys in my pants pocket—waiting for the lady to appear. This time my plan was to wait until she got in the elevator and then go to the stairway right outside my front door, up the stairs to the second floor, and trust my luck to encounter her in the hall.

And there she was, fast-stepping it through the front gate, through the lobby, and to her mailbox. *Now, why didn't she go to the mailbox yesterday?* I mused that she was looking good enough to eat as I admired her in her yellow skirt and yellow-and-white diagonal-striped blouse. I saw her reach the elevator and push the call button, and I dashed out the front door and up the stairs, two at a time.

When I reached the second floor, I trotted down the long hallway and through two fire hazard doors and turned in the direction of the elevator. I slowed to a walk. I knew there was no guarantee that she would come this way, but if she did, I didn't want her to see me running. However, the thought that she could go in the opposite direction made me quicken my pace.

It hit me that she must have gone the opposite way after I went through the last two fire doors before the elevator and didn't see her. I began trotting again, past the elevator, got a whiff of perfume, and then saw a fire hazard door up ahead slowly closing. I darted through it in time to hear one of the six apartment doors down the long hallway close.

I must have buzzard's luck, I mused. *Can't kill nothing, and won't nothing die.*

At a more normal pace, I headed toward the next fire door, hoping to hear something. Just as I passed apartment 253 on my right, I heard a lock click.

Gotcha! I thought elatedly.

On returning to the first floor via the elevator, I went directly to the mailboxes and noted that apartment 253 belonged to an M. Handley, and that mailbox was definitely in the vicinity of where I had seen her bending the other day. *It had to be her.*

Anyway, I knew that I had to wait until Monday to make another attempt at her, since the next day was Saturday. The closer I came to possibly meeting her, the more anxious I got. It was going to be a long weekend.

I awoke the next morning to the sounds of female voices and splashing water. I leaped out of my king-sized bed and went to the window. There were six bikini-clad cuties lying around the pool, soaking up the bright eighty-degree sun: two Asians, three Blacks, and one White. Three other girls and two guys were in the water, splashing each other. None were M. Handley of Apartment 253.

Just as I was heading to the bathroom to take a shower, my intercom buzzed. I looked out my bedroom window and saw Beau Arceneaux, one of my girl-chasing ex-army buddies and employees, at the front gate. He lived a block up the street.

"Come around to the patio door," I told him over the call box in the living room. Moving to the sliding door, I saw him approaching, almost bumping into a table as he was busy watching the cuties around the pool.

"You'd better look where you going or go where you're looking," I joked as I slid open the door.

"What's happenin', Doctor?" Beau greeted as he stepped into the living room. Everyone was "Doctor" to him.

"You got it. What's the word?"

"Just you, me, and Jesus," he replied customarily. "Got any vegetables?"

"Hmmph. Yeah, the same stuff you left over here four months ago," I reminded him. "Just look in the box under the end table. Help yourself; it's yours anyway. There's some brew in the fridge. I'm gonna take a quick shower."

Beau was laid back on my soft black leather couch with his feet propped up on the cocktail table next to the shoebox and a pack of E-Z Widers when I emerged from the bathroom in my floor-length striped robe. He had a joint in one hand and a beer in the other.

"Hey, man, get yo' feet off my table!" I yelled as I went into the bedroom to dress. "What are *you* doing up so early anyway? It's only ten o'clock."

"Man, I haven't been to bed yet," he answered. "You know I don't need no sleep on the weekends."

"Where'd you go last night?"

"To the Onion, of course." He seemed to perk up at the memory of it. The Onion was a Mexican restaurant and bar in the office building next to the building we worked in. It was actually named "the Red Onion"; we had shortened it to "the Onion." At night, the bar section turned into a nightclub. "My luck has been too good there to change now. I picked up this chick. When the club closed, we went to breakfast, and after that we wound up at the beach. We were gettin' high, and I just *knew* I was gon' be gittin' some of her soul food, heh heh."

"Hear hear for the soul food." I laughed. "So how was it?"

"How was what?"

"The soul food, fool."

"Oh, I, uh … I didn't get it."

"You didn't get it?"

"Didn't get it."

"Why? What happened?"

"Passed out."

"*She* passed out!"

"Nope."

"Man, don't tell me you didn't get the order because you were too high."

Silence.

"Well?" I asked from the bedroom.

"Well what?"

"Did you?"

"Hey, you said don't tell you."

"Give me a break," I said as I got a brew from the fridge, completely dressed. "No, better yet, give me a *brick*."

"She talked about me like a dog as she drove me back over here," Beau related, dragging on the joint. "Called me less than a man. A stone cutie too. I'll make it up to her."

"What was her name?"

"Huh?"

"Her name?"

"Uh, let's see ... I got it here somewhere," he responded, going through his pockets. "Now, where did I put it?"

"Beau."

"I know it's here somewhere ... with her number."

"Beau!"

"Now, what did I do with it?"

"Beau?"

"Let me think."

"*Beau!*"

"Huh!"

"Did you ask her for it?"

"Hmm, you know what?"

"What?"

"I can't remember."

"Chalk another one up for you, Beau."

"Hell, my luck's so good at the Onion that I can find another one just as fine or finer tonight. Wha'chu gettin' into tonight?"

"I have *no* idea," I admitted. "I'll just play it by ear."

"I can dig that. So what's the word on that chick you've been talking about all week—the one who lives here."

"Oh, I'm, uh, just biding my time with her."

"What's her name, again?"

"Huh."

"Her name?"

"Uh …"

"I know you got it by now, as fast as you work."

"Naw, man, I didn't get it yet. I'm just going to play it slow. I'll meet her in due time."

"So will a lot of other dudes," Beau said pointedly. "Why don't you just go ahead and give the party, Doctor?"

He and a few others had been hounding me about throwing a party for a few weeks now. I'd thought about it but kept putting it off. Maybe this would be a good way to meet Apartment 253 and other cuties in the building.

"Okay, you know what? I'm going to do it. It's on," I agreed.

"It's on?"

"It's on!" I repeated. "Now, I'll do all the inviting. I want at least three ladies for every one guy, but not a whole lot of guys—just our close friends and any new CODs we know, including the ladies in this complex."

"When?"

"Two weeks from today should be enough time," I calculated.

"All right then." Beau jumped up and headed out the door with a big smile on his face. "It's on! I'll holler at you later."

"*I'll* do the inviting, Beau," I reiterated as he closed the door behind him.

"Yeah, yeah, no problem." With that, he was gone.

Beau was one of my boys, all right, but his taste in women left something to be desired—such as *better* taste. He seemed to be turned on by the skankiest babes. He'd been that way in the army too. Class didn't seem to mean a thing to him. I think it was the weed that made him like that. A day was not complete to him if he didn't get a chance to hit a joint or two. And if he was lucky, he would find some coke to snort also.

I wasn't like that. No drugs for me. Beau had left the weed there a few months earlier; it was just a little bit. I guess he was so high that he totally forgot that he had left it behind. I was never one to sit around by myself smoking a joint, but I kept it there in case I ever had company of the female persuasion who might want to dabble. Just trying to be a good host.

Anyway, I didn't want Beau inviting any of his skanks to my party. I knew I had to try to monitor him for the next two weeks. He didn't have a phone at home, because he could never keep his phone bill paid. So if he was going to do any inviting, he would probably use the office phones to make his personal calls, which he had been doing for a while now.

I made up some flyers at work and passed them out to a few cuties in the office building, plus some of the cool brothers. I invited a private investigator named Born Luckey. Also, I told Doctor Joseph Holliday, whose dental office was in the building. He was a down-to-earth brother. He said he'd bring his friend, Daniel Dabineau, to the party. I didn't know that a couple of years later Doc, Dab, and I would become best friends and roommates at the Mini-Mansion.

During this period, I didn't know a lot of guys in LA—mainly the guys that worked for me, Beau and Ed, plus my business partner, George, and my three college buddies, Claude Longley, Dennis Elliot, and Douglas Kenner. Claude, Doug, and I were like brothers; Denn was like a first cousin. Later Doc and Dab became like siblings too.

Also I invited a group of guys I met through Claude. He, Doug, and I became friends in college because we liked to play pinochle, which I had learned to play in the army. The guys Claude met here in LA were also pinochle players. In fact, we started playing once a week on Tuesday, rotating locations. We all became tight friends too.

That was it for the men I invited to the party—except, of course, for the miscellaneous guys who probably would respond to the flyers I slipped under each door in the apartment complex. In fact, I slipped one under M. Handley's door and slipped another into her mailbox to make sure she got it. I had given up on trying to intercept her in the hallway. I was hoping the party would make her come to me.

The day of the party arrived. Beau came by early to help out, along with Claude, Doug, and Beverly, my receptionist at the office. Born Luckey came by early also, to mix a concoction that he had told me about that consisted of wine, rum, and punch. We put it into two water bottles and replaced the water bottle in my Sparkletts water cooler with the rum punch bottle.

The party jumped off. Folks were arriving in clumps. My large one-bedroom apartment was bursting at the seams. I unlocked the patio door, and some of the guests spilled out there until neighbors complained about the noise and I had to get everyone back inside.

About two hours into the party, the cops came by. They asked for the resident of the unit to step out into the hall.

I did.

"Your party's too loud, sir," one of the officers announced. "Many called to complain. Tone it down. If we should come back, we're going to shut down the party. Okay?"

"Many? How many?" I asked.

"It doesn't matter how many. *One* is too many. Just tone it down. okay, sport?"

"Okay," I said.

I went back inside and turned down the music and took the bass out of it. But the party continued. There were lots of ladies there—a lot of new faces I hadn't seen before and some that I knew and had invited, including some of the best-looking applicants that had come through my employment agency. But there was no M. Handley from Apartment 253.

I could tell which of the females were my invitees and which were Beau's. The gum-chewing, Jheri-curled, Lee-Press-On-Nails-wearing chicks were his. The mud ducks. All the others were mine.

At one point, there was a long line waiting for the restroom. Doug informed me that Claude had taken a lady in there and was probably getting busy, holding up everyone. I had to discreetly get him out of there.

Claude Longley had been doing that at parties since our college days together in DC. That's why I had devised a way of unlocking the bathroom door from the outside. I shooed him and his mud duck out of there, to the applause of everyone else in line.

The rum punch mix was potent. They were drinking it like Kool-Aid and losing control of their minds, dancing all over the place, turning the music back up, eating anything they could find, breaking some of my dishes, and yelling at the tops of their lungs. I even had to break up a potential fight.

"Davey, come here, man." Beau beckoned to me. He was in the corner, talking to a young lady. She looked pretty good, for Beau's taste. "Tell him what you told me."

"Hi, I'm Jenny," the girl began. "I live here in the building. Thanks for inviting us, by the way."

"You're welcome," I replied.

"C'mon, tell him," insisted Beau.

"What?" I asked.

"Well, I was in the laundry room downstairs a few days ago," she related, "talking to this lady. We were down there for a long while just shooting the breeze, and I mentioned your party here in 105. She said that someone had pointed out the guy who lives in 105 to her and she was looking forward to meeting him, but she told me she's kind of shy and didn't know if she would come to the party."

"What was this lady name?" I asked.

"You know, I don't remember her name," she admitted. "I just know that she lives in apartment 253."

253! That's M. Handley. She's talking about M. Handley!

"A pretty girl," Jenny continued. "Very good looking, but quiet. She seems like the kind that don't like to put her business in the streets."

Like you're doing now, I thought. "Thanks for the info, Jenny," I said. "Enjoy the party."

So this probably means that she's not coming, I told myself. *The lady I'm interested in and who apparently is interested in me—the lady who is the reason for me giving this party—is not coming?* I decided to keep hope alive. I went to the water cooler and refilled my glass with the punch.

The cops came again.

"Mr. Stein," the cop said after I had stepped back out into the hallway, "we don't want to shut you down, but I promise you, if we get one more call, many or not, it's over, sport. Just keep the music down."

I must admit, this cop may not be an English major with his adjective misuse, but he is giving me a break. I was surprised that they gave me another chance. I guess LAPD *could* be nice to Black folks—sometimes. And these were two White cops.

I went back in and turned down the music again, telling the guests that many of the neighbors were complaining so they had to enjoy themselves quietly. The party had started at nine o'clock, and it was now midnight. Three hours, and M. Handley was a no-show. But it was one hell of a party.

I did get a couple of phone numbers from two of the new cuties in the assemblage, but they were just so-so—nothing to write home about. My reason for having the party was in hopes of finally meeting M. Handley, a long letter home in the making. So although it was a fun party, I was still disappointed, and I was getting more disappointed the later it got.

I deliberately turned up the music.

Twenty minutes later, there was a knock at my door.

"Mr. Stein, your party's over," the stern cop declared. "We got that third call from many. Please tell your guests to leave in an orderly fashion."

I kept the door open as I made the announcement to my guests. They protested but started filing out, giving the officers dirty looks.

As Dab and Doc were leaving, they complimented me on the party and invited Doug, Claude, Denn, and me to a party that another doctor in Doc's neighborhood in Fox Hills was giving the following weekend.

Doug, Claude, and Beau were the last to walk out.

"I'll talk to you guys tomorrow," I told them.

"Mr. Stein, you have a nice night," the policemen said as they departed after they made sure the party was over.

I looked over my place after everyone was gone. It was a mess. Half-full paper plates and cups were everywhere, liquid was on the floor, the trash can was overflowing, and a full trash bag was on the floor in the kitchen. I didn't know where to start. I turned on some jazz, really low.

There was a knock on the door.

"Hello!" I answered.

"I'm here for the party."

"The party's over!" I called out.

The knock came again.

"The party's over!" I repeated.

Again a knock. *This person can't hear,* I realized.

I went closer to the door and repeated, "The party's over!"

The knock came again.

I flung the door open, saying, "The party's o—"

There stood M. Handley of apartment 253.

"Is the party over?" she asked with a smile.

"No!" I quickly replied, motioning her in. "Well, the party *was* over, but c'mon in."

I was surprised that she showed up so late and knocked on my door even though there was no loud party music, but I was glad she did. The girl was looking *good,* and she even had a bottle of champagne in her hand.

She handed me the champagne. "For you," she said as she presented it.

"Thank you." I accepted it. "Want some?"

"Yes, please."

I directed her to sit on one of the barstools while I got a couple of flutes out and popped the cork. "My name is Davey, by the way," I introduced.

"Hi, Davey," she responded, "I'm Minnie."

"Hi, Min—" I stopped. "Minnie?" I recalled the cops and the three calls they got. *They were saying "Minnie," not "many,"* I realized.

She smiled.

"Minnie!" I said, looking at her. Her smile broadened. I smiled.

"Minnnnnn-neeeeeee!" I chuckled. "Shy, discreet Minnie." I nodded my head knowingly as I poured the champagne into two flutes and we clinked glasses.

Yeah, the party most definitely wasn't over.

BLIND LEADING
THE BLIND ... ON

IF YOU'RE ASTUTE, YOU CAN TELL A LOT FROM A VOICE OVER THE phone. You can tell whether a person is having a good day, whether a person is not feeling well, or whether a person is sad. You can tell whether a person has a sense of humor, and whether he or she is a sharp person or a positive person. You can even tell whether a person is smiling over the phone. But you can't tell what a person looks like.

I used to think I could. I thought I could definitely tell whether a female was a cutie pie—or, as we called them, a COD, which stood for "cutie on duty"—over the phone. I even thought I could tell whether a woman was fat or slender by her voice.

Wrong!

I had been speaking with a lady on the phone for about three months. In my business of running an employment agency, I talked to people all the time on the phone. And I talked to receptionists and secretaries more than I cared to. Some of them had great voices— sexy voices. Maybe that was a criterion for the job, because a great voice does put callers at ease—especially male callers. And that's when the friendly flirting begins.

Now, there's nothing wrong with friendly flirting. It's a way of establishing a rapport with someone you're attempting to do business with. This is a way to get them on your side and get them to open up to you.

I had been trying to get the foot of our agency, the Stein and Frank Agency, in the door with an affluent entertainment law firm in the high-class Century City area of Los Angeles for almost a year. A few months earlier, they—the Standifer Group—hired a new human resources assistant, and she was Black. Her name was Melody Brewer. Her voice was like a melody—sweet, soft, and sexy.

"HR," she answered after Becky, the receptionist, put me through to her.

"Good morning, Melody," I greeted in my best Barry White pitch. Of course I put a little more bass in my voice whenever I hear a female voice on the phone.

"Good morning, Davey," she replied in her melodic tone. "This is your lucky day."

"What?"

"We're going to be needing a new receptionist, and Ms. Granowski, my boss, asked me to try a couple of new agencies, and I thought about you."

"I appreciate that!"

"You do handle clericals, too, right?"

"Clerical, administrative, legal aid, attorneys, corporate, management trainees, sales—everything."

"Good. Well, Becky, gave us her two-week notice yesterday, so we're looking for someone to replace her ASAP."

"And I was just calling you to say hi," I lied. I *never* just call to say hi. Every time I dialed that number, I was hoping she would have a requisition for a job opening that she would share with me that would give me the opportunity to show her what our agency could do. I finally got a break. "Hold on. Let me get my pad. Usually I would have one of my employment consultants take the job order info from you, but since I have you on the phone and you're such good people, I'll jot down the requirements myself. Okay, shoot."

"Well, you know, just the basic stuff. She must be able to type seventy words per minute, know ten-key by touch, have at least three years of experience working a PBX system, be familiar with legal terminology, be sharp, be a go-getter, be personable, be a nonsmoker, and, of course, good FOA. We'll start her off somewhere between six hundred and seven hundred a week, depending on experience. And you know we have profit-sharing, 401(k), and tuition reimbursement, and there're growth opportunities."

"How important is FOA?" I knew the answer but was creating small talk as I made notes.

"Front office appearance is *very* important," Melody shared. "When clients enter our suite, they need to see an attractive, well-dressed face greeting them right away. Puts them at ease."

"That's true." I chuckled. "Now, six hundred to seven hundred a week for a receptionist?"

"We're a top law firm. We pay good money for *top* people. That's why Becky stayed here so long. Heck, that's why I'm here."

"Well, go 'head on with yo' bad self."

"You don't hear me, tho'."

"Too near you to hear you." I laughed. "Anything else?"

"Well, uh, yes." Her voice got lower. "Just between you, me, and the bedpost, uh, we'd like a minority—a Black if possible."

I knew that was hard for her to tell me. And I also knew that it was because of the rapport that we had established that she took the chance to tell me that. It's not something she could tell the other agencies that she dealt with. It was a definite no-no to specify a specific race, but it was a yes-yes for me, since 70 percent of my applicants were minorities. Melody shared that tidbit with me because of our telephone friendship, I realized, and to give me a leg up on my competitors.

Finally I was getting my chance to impress the Standifer Group with the quality of candidates we could supply. I knew they did a lot of hiring in the three offices they had here in Southern California. My partner and I coveted their business. We wanted to be on their PAL—their preferred agencies list.

"Thank you, Melody," I said sincerely, "I really do appreciate the opportunity. We'll get on it right away, keeping *all* your specifications in mind."

"Good, and you're welcome, Davey dear. You see? All your phone calls finally paid off."

"Well, all my calls weren't about just doing business with you guys. I just like hearing your voice."

"And I like yours too. How tall are you, by the way?"

"Six four."

"Yeah, right. You sound like you're five seven."

"How can you tell a guy's height from his voice?"

"Because you sound like someone I know, and that someone is five feet seven."

"Do you like short men?"

"No, I like them over six feet."

"I tell you what, I've been wondering what you look like too. So why don't we just meet after work today for a drink, and then you can *see* how tall I am."

"I'm game," she consented, "but tomorrow is better for me."

"That'll work. We'll talk tomorrow, and you tell me when and where. Cool?"

"Cool. You have a nice day."

"I will. You too. And I'm already looking forward to tomorrow."

We hung up, and I gave the new job requisition to my crew of employment counselors. They jumped right on it. I knew we had some *good-looking*, talented Black candidates that could fill that position. Then I thought about the position I wanted to fill.

Melody's sexy voice had been turning me on for months now as we openly flirted with each other. In previous conversations, she told me how she liked to turn a man on with her cooking, how she liked to give massages, and how she could hold her own when it came to talking about sports. She admitted that she was looking for a good man that she could get to know and fall in love with. She said she believed in love at first sight.

Conversely, I told her that I liked taking a woman out to eat at fine restaurants, that I liked washing a woman's hair, that I wasn't involved but was looking for a good lady, and that I was a part-owner of the agency.

I hadn't wanted to give her too much info about me, because I didn't know if our relationship would change after I met her. If she was not a COD, she would just remain a business acquaintance, and the info she had would be all she would get. If she turned out to be girlfriend material, I would share more intimate details about me and my life.

I knew Dab and Doc would have their opinions about my rendezvous. They were very opinionated.

When I first moved into the Mini-Mansion, there were four of us. Dab, Doc, and Douglas "Doug" Kenner were known as the 3Ds. I, Davey Stein, became the fourth D, so that's what our friends called us. However, Doug was getting married soon and was moving out, so the 4Ds were going to be the 3Ds again. Also, we all were involved in promoting a new nightclub in Beverly Hills on Friday nights that was coincidentally called Rendezvous.

"You see, you told her too much," Dab said as he, Doc, and I sat in the den watching an NBA Playoff game. "She knows that you got some dough and like spending it on women."

"Yeah," added Doc, "and you don't even know what she looks like. She might turn out to be a mud duck."

"She don't sound like no mud duck," I informed him.

"Sound don't mean shit." Dab laughed. "You said that you sounded five feet seven to her."

"That's true," I said.

"And didn't you say she told you that she likes to cook?" Dab continued.

"Yeah."

"Well, if she likes to cook, she likes to *eat*," Dab deducted. "I bet she's fat."

"Davey, you might want to rethink this meeting-ski," Doc suggested.

Dab laughed again. "Or have a plan B in case she turns out to be an F."

"Yeah, before you meet," offered Doc, "tell her that you have somewhere else to be at a certain time. But if she turns out to be a COD, just tell her you cancelled it."

"Hmmm … that might work."

"It's either that or take the chance that you'll be spending a couple of hours with an ug-mo." Dab was enjoying this.

"Yep," Doc added, "and then your rep as the guy who only dates tens will be out the window-ski."

"I ain't worried about no rep," I fibbed.

"Yeah, right," Dab scoffed.

⌒

The next day, I waited until just before lunch to call Melody.

"Hey, Davey," she greeted when she came on the line. "Are we still on for after work?"

"Definitely," I assured her. "Where do you want to meet?"

"Let's meet at Georgia's over on Melrose."

"Oh, I've been there. It's just west of La Brea, right?"

"Exactly," she confirmed. "How about six o'clock?"

"Six is fine."

"Now, how will I know you?"

"Well, I'm six four and I have on a gray suit today," I told her, looking at my reflection in the window overlooking the 3600 block of Wilshire in my black suit.

"Okay, and I'm five six, and I'll have on a navy-blue business suit with a pink blouse."

"Got it. I'll see you at six."

I had decided not to listen to Dab and Doc. I wanted to do this my way. They were right about one thing, though; I did have a reputation to uphold. But I didn't want to hurt anyone's feelings with some lame excuse of having other plans. The woman I had been flirting with on the phone for a few months was sharp enough to see through that. So, by doing it my way, I could protect myself, and her feelings, with a lie. If she turned out to be a COD, I'd say that she had misunderstood and that I had said *charcoal-gray* suit, which is a *lighter* black.

Georgia's was a relatively new restaurant bar on Melrose in West Hollywood. It was owned by Norm Nixon, formerly of the LA Lakers;

his wife, Debbie Allen; Brad Johnson, an acquaintance of Dab's from New York; and Denzel Washington. I lucked out and found parking on Melrose and entered behind three fine sisters. All three were dressed in yellow, albeit three different shades of yellow.

Ordinarily I would have flirted with them, but I was on a mission today.

There were two bars in the establishment; one was to the left of the main entrance, and the other to the right, where the main dining area was. Sandwiched between the two was a spacious lounge area. The place was fairly crowded for a Wednesday evening.

The three ladies split up. Two went to the main area, and the one in a yellow polka-dot dress went to the smaller bar to the left.

I followed the two into the main bar area. They grabbed a table for four. I went straight to the bar, ordered a cuba libre with Myers's rum, and looked around as the bartender prepared my drink. Sometimes I could find Denzel sitting at the bar in the main area. I had actually chatted with him once there. Nice brother.

Just then, a lady in a navy-blue suit and pale pink blouse walked in and glanced around as if looking for someone.

Aw, shit! I cursed under my breath. *Is that Melody? Please don't be.*

She was a redbone, about five three with chubby cheeks and cornrows. She had to weigh way over two hundred pounds. I did not date short women or women who weighed more than me. She looked in my direction and wobbled toward the bar. I immediately left my credit card with the bartender and deserted the area. I headed for the other bar, passing right by her.

The smaller bar was fairly crowded also. I noticed the very attractive sister in the yellow polka dots sitting at the bar. Damn, talk about COD! This lady was off the charts. Her legs were crossed as she sat there on the barstool, sipping her drink. And a great pair of legs they were. But I was trying to figure out what I was going to do about the lady in the navy-blue suit. I took a gulp of my drink as my eyes casually roamed the room.

That's when I spotted another lady clad in navy blue with a frilly hot-pink blouse sitting alone at a table. Her outfit was a pantsuit. This one wasn't fat, but she also wasn't anywhere near attractive. In fact, she was further from attractive than the fat lady wearing navy blue in the main area. She was bug-eyed, had a wide nose, and had on a wig that wasn't anywhere near flattering. She looked at me and smiled. Her gold tooth sparkled as a ray of sunlight hit it.

Aw hell no, I silently cursed again. Thank God I had lied about what I was wearing.

There was no way that I was going to approach either of the two in navy blue to find out which one was Melody. I realized that I might jeopardize my business with the law firm, but I didn't want to go through the motions of pretending that I was interested and end up hurting her feelings further down the road. The best way out of this, I decided, was to call her later and say that something came up and I never made it to Georgia's.

With that in mind, I figured that I should get out of the place as soon as I could, just in case someone I knew happened to show up and said my name out loud. But before I left, I wanted to say something to the COD in yellow at the bar. I looked at her and smiled. She smiled back.

As I navigated my way between the tables to go and buy her a drink, the guy who was sitting a few stools down from her saw me approaching and quickly made his move. He got up and moved down to occupy the empty stool next to her. I saw him introduce himself to her as he looked at me out of the corner of his eye. She gave him the same gorgeous smile that she had given me.

Oh well, you snooze, you lose, I thought as I continued past them back to the main bar to retrieve my credit card. The fat chick in navy blue was sitting at the far end of the bar, chatting with a skinny, nerdy-looking guy with glasses in a gray suit.

Was she Melody and did she think he was me?

As soon as I got outside, I burst out laughing. *Hell, what am I laughing at?* I thought. *She caught. I was the one leaving alone.* I laughed even harder.

⌐⌐⌐⌐⌐

The next day, I waited until midafternoon before I called the Standifer Group. I was surprised when Becky, the receptionist, told me that Melody had called out for the day.

Damn, I thought, *she was so disappointed that she couldn't go to work.* Then I considered the guy in the gray suit, wondering whether he could've been of ill repute and had Melody tied up somewhere. *But, no,* I thought, *Becky said she had called out, so she has to be okay. I'll call her tomorrow.*

Friday, I dialed the law firm again and asked for Melody's extension, only to be told by Becky that she had taken another day off.

This girl is ducking me, I figured. I realized that she must have known who I was at Georgia's and that she was upset about my deception and, consequently, was evading me. She probably was embarrassed by the fact that I had been so turned off by her appearance that I stooped to such drastic means to avoid her. I decided to leave her alone for a while.

Over the weekend, I berated myself for my duplicity with Melody, but I made no effort to call her on Monday.

Tuesday afternoon I received a call from her.

"Davey, dear," she began cheerfully, "how are you?"

"Uh, fine," I was hesitant because I didn't know where this call was going. I was picturing her in her navy-blue business suit. I just didn't know what face to use in the picture—the redbone face with cornrows or the bug-eyed face with the unflattering wig. "How are *you* doing?" I asked, testing the waters.

"I'm doing great," Melody replied enthusiastically. "Two things. Well, three really. I like two of the candidates your office sent over. I want to arrange an interview for each. Do I talk to you?"

"No, but I'll have the counselors who submitted the candidates call you back as soon as they return from lunch to set up the interviews, because they know their applicants' schedules. Okay?"

"Great!" she agreed. "Now, the third thing. I don't know how to say this, but here goes. Uh, last, uh … last Wednesday was a little embarrassing."

"Yeah, I know, and I, uh … I want to apologize for telling you—"

"No, no," she interrupted, "*you* don't have to apologize. *I* should be the one apologizing." She was right. She should've told me she was a mutt. "I was going to explain when I saw you, but I, uh, thought about what my mother said about good manners and, uh …"

"Yeah, good manners," I broke in. "I expect good manners from others because usually I am mannerly, but, uh, I …"

"And well you should expect it," she agreed, "even if one is not mannerly."

"Is that why you were avoiding me last Thursday and Friday?"

"No, I wasn't avoiding you, even though *I* was definitely unmannerly Wednesday. I was just hanging out with the guy I met at Georgia's. In fact, we spent the whole weekend together in Palm Springs." I thought about the nerdy, glasses-wearing guy in the gray suit. "But I just wanted to apologize for my lack of manners by having the waitress give you that note when I was leaving with the guy. I should've walked over there and spoken to you, but you seemed to be having fun with that lady."

"What lady? What note?"

"The lady that you were talking to at the main bar. The light-skinned lady in the blue suit."

"Uh, that wasn't you?"

"Who? The plus-size lady? Hell no! You mean you didn't know that you were not talking to me?"

"Uh, that wasn't **me** talking to her."

"That wasn't you in the gray suit with glasses?"

"Uh, no, that wasn't me. So, uh, where were you?"

"I was in the other bar area."

"Ah, yeah, I saw you," I admitted, thinking of how bad that wig looked.

"I didn't see you."

"You smiled at me," I stated, remembering the gold tooth shining.

"What did you have on?"

"A black, uh-ruh … I mean, a charcoal-gray suit with a red-and-gray tie."

"*That* was you? Tall, bald, great eyes and smile, with a goatee?"

"Yeah, that be me, I guess."

"Yes, you smiled and started toward me, until Henry beat you to the punch."

"Henry?"

"Yes, Henry, the guy I spent the last five days with. I told you I believe in love at first sight. He left his seat and came and sat next to me."

"At your table?"

"No, I wasn't at a table," she corrected matter-of-factly. "I was at the bar."

My eyes got wide.

"At the bar?"

"Yes, and that's what I'm apologizing for, for lying about what I was wearing that day. Very unmannerly of me."

"Uh, what *were* you wearing?"

"A yellow polka-dot dress," she said.

I think I sat there at my desk for a solid hour after we hung up repeatedly hitting my head with the phone's handset as I admonished myself, uttering, "That's what you get for being a big dummy, a big dummy, a big dummy."

SNEAK EASY

I FELT THE EXCITEMENT AS SOON AS I DROVE UP FOR HAPPY HOUR at the Speakeasy in West Hollywood. There was something about this club on Fridays after work. In fact, there was something about nightclubs, period, that put me in a rush. There was something about the possibilities that were available at a club on a given night.

New stuff.

For a single guy, it was always about meeting new stuff—a new, pretty, voluptuous, sexy, friendly, willing lady that one could meat. That's right—*meat*.

Of course, now, nightclubs are not the only way to meat new stuff. You can catch at supermarkets, shopping malls, libraries, gas stations, or just walking down the street. Nightclubs, however, offer a wider variety of prospects gathered in a spot conducive to meeting. And said prospects come with a more approachable attitude.

I did not go to the Speakeasy every Friday, but at least twice a month we made it our stop for happy hour. Plus, on this particular Friday, my roomies Dab and Doc wanted to start our evening out there before we hit some of the other LA hot spots. We were out honky-tonking. That's what they called nightclub hopping in the old days. This was before we started doing our own Friday-night club promotions at Rendezvous.

Back in the day, the Speakeasy was one of our favorite venues to go to for the honeys. Some Fridays were so-so, but if we caught the spot on the right Friday, it was like going to a candy store to shop for sweets. No hard candy, though; we craved the soft-centered variety.

And the "soft center" represented. A guy could stock up on phone numbers on a good Friday. And *this* Friday *was* Good Friday. It was Easter weekend. Folks had worked a half day, gone to the salons or barbershops to get their dos did, and now were ready to get their drink on. Plus the Ebony Fashion Fair was in town. Their show was Easter Sunday at the convention center. That meant that the ladies would be out and about this weekend.

I'd been seeing this girl, Renee, for a couple of months now, and she was getting a little too attached for my good, wanting me to go to boring events with her: art shows, classical music concerts, seminars on relationships, and stuff like that.

Don't get me wrong. I had nothing against being seen out with Renee, but I was a bachelor and still enjoying it at this point. I'd never called her my girl, my boo, my thing, my stuff, *my* nothing! We just spent a decent amount of time together, and I knew she wanted to put a label on it. But I didn't. I felt that I could still hang with the fellas, and she was supposed to be cool with that.

She wasn't that cool with that. But that was *her* problem. However, she knew better than to come at me about it with that hot temper of hers, because then I probably would stop meating her, and I didn't think she was ready for that.

In fact, Renee wanted me to come over this night before it got too late, but I told her I had some business to take care of and that I would come by a little later, but not "too late."

Women seem to want to make a statement when they think they have you hooked. Being with the dude in their life on Friday nights is a statement to womankind. However, I was the rebellious type. Doc always said that in a relationship, you're either the trainer or the trainee. I never wanted to be the trainee, so rebelling helped me check that. But, as I said, I *did* tell Renee that I would come by later. What I didn't disclose was that it depended on how the night went. What she didn't know was that she was plan B.

There were a few cars in front of me in line for the valet, and each car had women exiting it. I watched them as they emerged and headed into the club, two in one car, three in the next, five in the Seville directly in front of me. And they all looked good. *This is going to be a* good *Friday,* I thought.

I almost tripped over the valet's foot getting out of my ride; that's how anxious I was to get in there.

Our buddy Carl, the doorman, was at his post.

"Hey Davey," he greeted, waving me on through without collecting any money.

"What's up, Carl?"

"Your boys are in there."

"Yeah, I know. Thanks."

I went through the door and headed back to the main lounge area past the long, crowded bar on the right. I spotted Doc at a table in front of the cushioned booths that ran along the red-wallpapered walls. Apparently someone was celebrating something. There were multicolored balloons hanging overhead in the area.

"Davey, it's Shelia's birthday today," Doc told me as I walked up to the table.

"Where is she?" I asked, looking around. There were several familiar faces sitting at the booth with a birthday cake on the table. I saw Sheila's boyfriend, Cornell Dill, among the group. They all waved.

"She just went to the bathroom," Doc said. "Grab a seat-ski, man."

I pulled an empty chair over and sat just as our favorite waitress, Dot, came by.

"I know, I know, cuba libre, Myers's rum, tall," she rattled off. "You and your roommate, Doug, are the only ones who ever order that drink."

"Ex-roommate," I corrected. "Remember: he got married. Plus he's a big-time TV star now," I said, giving Doug Kenner his props.

"It's Cutie-Pie City in here tonight, man," Doc informed as Dot moved on.

"I see," I said. "Where's Dab?"

"You just walked past him. He's over there at the bar-ski," Doc said and then chuckled, "trying to talk to the lightest-skinned woman in here."

"That's our boy," I acknowledged with a chuckle.

I looked over at the bar I had just passed and saw Dab at the far end, standing next to an attractive slender lady dressed in white. There were two other good-looking ladies next to her who appeared to be with her. They were all smiling as Dab engaged the one in conversation and paid for the drinks that the bartender placed in front of the four of them. Then they all headed in our direction.

"These are the fellas," Dab told the three newcomers as they reached us. "Fellas, these are the ladies. Introduce yourselves." He directed them to sit at the table for four next to ours.

Knowing Dab, I knew he probably couldn't remember any of the ladies' names. This was his way of being refreshed with that information. Doc caught on too.

"Ladies, I'm Doc; that's Davey," Doc introduced.

"I'm Beverly," the lady in white said, "and this is Donna and Terri."

"You're a doctor?" Terri asked Doc.

"A dentist," he replied, handing her a business card.

"I might have to call you," she flirted.

"I might have to answer your call," he flirted back.

"Hey, Davey!" Sheila greeted, returning to the booth from the restroom.

I stood to give her a hug.

"Hey, birthday girl," I said. "What are you drinking?"

Sheila was one of those ladies that we all knew but wouldn't hit on even though she was a cutie—although she was a little too thick for me. We didn't come on to her because she was dating a guy that we all knew and liked. So although she wasn't with that guy any longer, we treated her like a sister. Dab had made overtures at her once or twice in the past, but Dab made overtures at all the good-looking ladies, regardless of who they were with. That's just him. He said he was just feeling them out, seeing where their heads were. We knew where he *wanted* their heads to be.

Sheila's new boyfriend, Cornell, was a cool brother, too, although his gear was always a little different from everyone else's; he had style. I've never heard anyone say a disparaging word about him. Plus the ladies liked him because he loved to dance, especially salsa.

"Apple martini," Sheila said. "I'm getting drunk tonight. By the way, y'all, Vanessa should be showing up soon to celebrate with me."

"Vanessa!" the three of us said in unison.

Vanessa was the middle sister in a family of three foxes. The trio had been coming to our Mini-Mansion parties and other functions that we'd given for a few years now. All three were glamorous. The three siblings all stood about five feet ten inches and were hourglass-figured redbone ladies who were very friendly and well liked by all the men. And yet no one was known to have been with any of them.

Vanessa and her older sister, Venita, were the two who partied with us the most. And although Venita was a stunning lady in her own right, she couldn't compare to Vanessa. Vanessa was beyond belief. She looked like a Black Barbie doll with her long, wavy dark brown hair; big brown eyes; and a smile that could melt an iceberg. She looked like Jayne Kennedy back in her heyday. I'm sure that I wasn't the only one who fantasized about being with her.

However, no one openly approached either of them. It was as though the men in the clique were afraid of getting shot down by them and, thus, being ridiculed by everyone else if the word got out. Plus no one wanted to jeopardize his friendship with the beauties.

And so, just knowing them, just having them come up and hug a brother whenever they ran into him in public, was satisfactory to the guys. That kind of acknowledgment from Vanessa, Venita, and Vivian, the youngest sibling, seemed to raise the huggee's esteem, making him beam as though he'd just hit the lotto.

"I thought she moved to Chicago," Doc recalled. "She's back in town-ski?"

"Yeah," Sheila said, "she's modeling with the Ebony Fashion Fair, you know."

"Is that why she left town?" I queried.

"Yeah," Sheila replied. "She applied several months ago, and they called her a couple of months later to come to Chicago and audition. They hired her on the spot."

"Right on-ski. Good for her," declared Doc.

"Fellas, we ought to go to the show Sunday to show our support," Dab suggested.

There goes Dab again, trying to impress the three new ladies, I realized.

"That's a good idea," I agreed. "Hook it up for us."

"Holliday, call tomorrow," Dab said, delegating as he always did. "Get the info, time, price, and all that so that we can check it out."

"It was *your* idea-ski," Joseph "Doc" Holliday balked, as he always did before giving in to Dab's dominant personality. "*You* call them."

"C'mon, man, you know I got that meeting tomorrow," Dab responded. "Davey?"

"I'm busy all day tomorrow," I lied. *Oh, hell naw, I ain't about to help him impress the ladies.*

"C'mon, Holliday," Dab beseeched, "you ain't doing nothing. Don't you want to support Vanessa?" He liked using the guilt approach to get one to give in to his biddings.

"All right, all right," Doc gave in, "I'll get the info."

I noticed that the three girls were trying to suppress their amusement.

"What are you guys up to?" I asked with a smile.

"We're *with* the Ebony Fashion Fair," Beverly said. "I'm one of the makeup artists, Donna's the stylist, and Terri works with wardrobe."

"We were invited here to the club tonight by Vanessa," Terri added.

"She had to go home and get her car first," Donna informed.

"And because Dan here was so nice, we were going to give you guys complimentary tickets for the show Sunday," Beverly said. Then she whispered, "Vanessa is hooking up Sheila and a guest as a birthday gift."

"Well, all right then!" I exclaimed. "Your next drinks are on me!"

"I've got them covered," Dab said, motioning for Dot to come over.

He always had to be the benevolent one in the group. I didn't know if his need to impress ladies had to do with his height—he was five feet, ten inches—or if it had to do with his complexion. He told us once how hard he had had it as a child because of him being the black—literally—sheep of the family.

We always let him have his moments in public, but we called him on it when no one else was around. That was Dan "Dab" Dabineau's MO. He would always showboat with the big baller approach and then later complain to us that he'd spent two or three hundred dollars more than he'd intended to on drinks and food for the ladies on a given night, as if we'd asked him to do it. But we were like brothers; we could do stuff like that. The bottom line was that we always had each other's back. It was one for all and all for one. That's why we were the 3Ds.

I felt a murmur in the club.

Two tall beauties with long, wavy hair had entered. All the men were staring in their direction. The bar area was crowded, but folks parted like the Red Sea as the pair strolled sexily from the entrance past the bar to the area we were in. They both had on form-fitting black dresses that clung like skin, hugging them like long-lost lovers. They hugged the perky breasts, small waists, flared hips, apple bottoms, tapered thighs, and long, shapely legs that were sandwiched between sandy black hair and black pumps. The two looked around with smiling exotic faces that could make a man want to rob a bank while brandishing a balled fist as his only weapon.

When they saw us, their smiles got broader. We all were smiling too.

Sheila was shaking her head while laughing. "You two oughta quit," she said as she stood to hug Vanessa and Venita.

"What?" Vanessa asked innocently, as if she weren't aware of the reactions they caused from the men in the club, as well as some of the women.

"Look who's here," Venita said to Vanessa when she noticed Dab, Doc, and me at our table in front of Sheila's booth. She came over to hug us.

"Wow," Vanessa exclaimed when she saw us with her three coworkers. "Dan, Doc, Davey, it's good to see you guys!" She came over and took her turn after Venita finished hugging us all.

Did I notice an extra squeeze from her when she got to me? I pondered.

"I see y'all met my girls," continued Vanessa. "I shoulda known you would. Girls, these are the brothers I told you about—the guys who gives the nice parties and do the nightclub promotions."

"You're the guys? The 3Ds?" Donna asked. "On our way to LA she bragged on you guys. Especially you," she added, looking at me.

"Me?" I was caught off guard.

Vanessa broke in quickly, giving Donna a quick look. "Don't listen to her."

"Oh, okay," I replied with a frown. *What's going on here?* I mused.

I, like all the other fellas, was infatuated with Vanessa and had considered hitting on her a couple of years ago, but I never did because we all had become such good partying friends. She, Venita, and Vivian felt more like sisters than anything else. Plus I felt that every guy she met probably hit on her at one time or another on the sly. I didn't want to be added to that list.

"What are you guys drinking?" I asked when I saw Dot bringing the drinks Dab had ordered for the three Fashion Fair girls.

Dab spoke up. "I got it covered."

Speaking of sly ones. I laughed inwardly. *And he was still trying to "feel them out."*

Vanessa and Venita sat in two chairs on the outer edge of Sheila's booth, which placed them close to our table and Vanessa's coworkers' table.

Now, I ain't no dummy. I had a female friend tell me on more than one occasion that I seemed to be oblivious of women flirting with me. She had said she noted several incidents when she had seen me at fundraising business meetings or out at clubs, and ladies were practically throwing themselves at me, she claimed, and I wasn't aware of it.

I told her that if I wasn't aware, it was probably because the ladies were not to my liking. But I later realized she was right and some *were* to my liking. Thus, I had decided to be more conscious of all women around me and not just lock onto the ones who caught my eye but be aware of the ones whose eyes *I* caught. Sometimes I regressed.

Vanessa? Is something up with her? I wondered.

"So how do you like being a Fashion Fair model?" I asked her across the table.

"I love it," she gushed. "When Sheila talked me into applying months ago, I just did it to shut her up. But when they called me a few months later and asked me to come to Chicago for the tryout, I was in shock. And then when they told me that I had been selected, I couldn't believe it."

"Believe it, girl," Beverly added. "Vanessa is one of the best models in the show."

"And very professional," Terri added.

Sheila beamed. "That's my girl!"

"By the way, She-She, these are for you." Vanessa pulled a gold envelope out of her purse and handed it to her friend. Sheila squealed when she saw the two VIP tickets it held.

"Thank you, thank you!"

"Happy birthday, She-She. You're the reason I'm with the show."

"That was very nice of you," I commended Vanessa.

"You guys are invited too," she informed us.

"Yeah, I told them that we will comp them," Beverly interjected.

"No, I already got them covered," Vanessa said. "They're going to be at the same table as Sheila, Cornell, and Venita, but I didn't know you guys were going to be here; I have your tickets at the hotel."

"We appreciate that," Dab said. His chair was closest to the two sisters. "I'll come by and get them tomorrow."

"I thought tomorrow you had a meeting-ski?" Doc queried, with a wink to me.

"It … it ain't, uh-ruh … it ain't, uh, all day," stuttered Dab.

"Uh-huh," Doc grunted.

"I feel like dancing!" Sheila shouted as the deejay played a current hit.

Doc grabbed her hand. "C'mon."

Dab reached for Beverly. Vanessa stood up, walked around the table, and took Cornell's hand.

"Dance with me," she uttered leading him toward the elevated dance floor behind the others.

"C'mon, Davey," Venita said to me, following behind the others. Both she and Vanessa loved to dance, I remembered.

The deejay played three fast songs back-to-back and then slowed it down. Venita and I were leaving the dance floor, as were a few others, when I felt a soft hand grab my hand. Surprised, I turned and saw Vanessa.

"Stay and dance with me," she urged.

Now you *know* I couldn't refuse. Like I said, I ain't no dummy.

"How long are you guys in town?" I asked as she stepped into my arms.

"Until Wednesday, and then we head for Oakland to do a show next Sunday."

"Must be fun."

"It is, although I miss LA and my friends and family here."

"I'm sure your friends and family miss you too."

"You think so?"

"Of course! Everyone misses you."

"Everyone?"

"Well, everyone who knows you."

"What about you?"

"Uh, what about me?"

"Nothing."

We were silent for a minute as the slow song continued. I felt her soft body up against mine, and before I knew it, I felt myself stiffening up.

"Uh, if you feel anything hard, it's my keys," I joked, "and if it moves, you're in trouble."

"It moved." Vanessa laughed.

"You're in trouble," I said matter-of-factly.

"I can handle it," she returned simply, looking me straight in my eyes.

She caught me off guard with that statement.

The song ended, and we returned to our seats. *Saved by the bell.*

The group of us stayed there at the Speakeasy for a few more hours. We went downstairs to partake of the tasty happy hour buffet prepared by the chef, Jimmy Santiago. Some of us played a hand or two of bid whist at the tables on the other side of the dance floor. We had champagne, birthday cake, and more drinks, and we were feeling good.

It was soon close to ten o'clock. Vanessa and I were on the dance floor again. An up-tempo song was playing this time. She danced up close to me.

"Listen," she whispered, "I'm going to take Venita on home and—"

"Okay," I interrupted, "we'll see you at the show Sunday, and maybe—"

"And then," she continued, "I'll be by your place."

"Oh, you're going to bring the tickets by tonight?" I asked, being the naive dummy that I was.

"I can, but that's not the reason I'm coming by. You're going to be there alone?"

"Uh, yeah," I responded, forgetting all about the fact that Renee was expecting me later.

"Davey, I've had a thing for you for a while now," she said, "but this has to be between you and me. No one else needs to know. Do you want me to come by?"

"Oh *hell* yeah!" I exclaimed.

"Okay then. We'll be leaving as soon as I get back to the table," she apprised. "And then I should be at your place in about a half hour. Okay?"

"Okay," agreed I. I couldn't believe my luck. *This girl who I've been fantasizing about for years is interested in me! She is coming by tonight to get with me! I'm going to be eating that pussy tonight! I'm gonna fuck Vanessa! I'm gonna rock her world!*

When we got back to our seat, Vanessa didn't even sit down.

She retrieved her purse from Venita, told everyone else good night, hugged Sheila, and left the club without a look back, brushing by guys trying to holler at her and Venita.

"So what you guys gonna do?" I asked the fellas, looking at my watch.

"Why don't we hang here a little longer," Dab suggested, "and then head down to Li'l J's." Everyone nodded in consent—except me.

"Man, I had a little too much to drink already, and I'm tired," I lied. "I'm gonna head on to the pad."

I couldn't wait to get out of there. Damn what they were going to do! I just wanted to make sure they weren't going to the house. I didn't want anyone to spook Vanessa. I wanted to honor her desire to keep our rendezvous hush-hush.

"All right," Doc said, "we'll see you at the pad-ski later."

"Yeah, *later*," I agreed. And I was out of there. I think they were still talking to me as I bolted to the valet. *Did I pay my tab?* I wondered. *Fuck it; the fellas will cover it.*

I bumped fists with Carl at the door, handed my ticket to the valet, and jumped into the car as soon as he drove up in it. The guy had to get out via the passenger side, climbing over the console while telling me the parking fee was five dollars.

"Keep the change," I yelled, as he scampered out with my ten-dollar bill in hand, looking bewildered.

It seemed like every damn red light was out to get me on LaCienega. I made a left on Third to take the La Brea route.

Bad move. There were some new clubs on Third, and folks were apparently just discovering them, because all of them were driving like they didn't know where the hell they were going; they were driving slowly, stopping, looking at their Thomas Bros. map books for directions, and calling out to pedestrians for help. I laid on my horn.

Vanessa said a half hour, dammit!

I had wanted to stop to get some champagne at the Liquor Bank but decided not to take that chance now. *Besides, Dab bought a bottle the other day. He won't mind if I borrow it. I'll buy him another.*

The traffic lights on La Brea were in cahoots with the lights on LaCienega, but finally I made it home with several minutes to spare.

I parked in the driveway, went in through the side door, and looked in the refrigerator to make sure that bottle of champagne was there. The house was looking good because the maid came every other Thursday.

Up to my room I headed, three stairs at a time. My bed was made. My black satin sheets and pillowcases were topped by a plush black comforter. I turned on the stereo and put in one of my smooth jazz tapes. I lit an Essence of Love incense stick and put it in the incense holder I'd bought in Jamaica. I placed it on top of my black chest of drawers. The exotic scent soon filled the room underneath the soft music. I turned off the overhead light and switched on the lamp near the balcony door.

The doorbell chimed.

I jetted out of my room to the top of the stairs and then nonchalantly sauntered down the steps, knowing that she could see me on the stairs through the glass center section of the front door.

"Hey you," she said with a smile as I opened the door.

"Hey you back at you," I returned. "C'mon in. Would you like some champagne?"

"Sure," she replied, following me into the kitchen that she knew so well from the many parties we'd given.

I retrieved two flutes from the cabinet and popped the cork. I filled both of our glasses, placed a spoon in the neck of the bottle, and put the bottle back in the refrigerator.

"What's that for?" she quizzed.

"To keep it from going flat," I enlightened. You can learn a lot on The Food Channel.

"Oh, I didn't know that."

"Let's go upstairs."

Vanessa smiled. "Let's."

I closed the door behind us as we entered my bedroom and motioned her toward the black leather love seat. I sat next to her.

"I can't believe that you're here with me." I turned to face her as I spoke.

"Finally."

"Finally?"

"Davey, I was digging on you when we first met you guys years ago. But you never made a play for me, so I didn't think you liked me. Then folks were saying that you guys were gay."

"What!"

"But I found out that that *definitely* wasn't true."

"They thought we were gay?"

"They were just hatin'. But several women vouched for *all* of you guys—and I do mean several. And I do mean *all*." She seemed to blush a little as she laughed.

"What do you mean, like testimonials?"

"Yeah, something like that, I guess. We were at a baby shower a couple of years ago—nothing but a bunch of women. You guys know most of them. And the ones y'all didn't know *wanted* to know y'all after some ladies told their stories about encounters with one or the other of you all."

"Damn, I wish I coulda been there, a fly on the wall."

"No, if you'd been there, you woulda gotten raped."

"Uh, like I said, I wish I coulda been there."

We both laughed.

"That's when I became even more intrigued by you," Vanessa admitted softly.

I set my drink on the black end table and reached for her chin. Our lips were just about to touch when there was a banging at my bedroom door.

"Davey!" It was Dab. "Did you open my champagne?"

What is he doing here! I got up and opened the door a crack. "Yeah, I did it. Don't worry about it," I whispered, blocking him from coming in.

"Don't worry about it!" His head was bobbing as he tried to peer into my room.

"Yeah, I'll get you another," I said, still whispering.

It seemed that the more I whispered, the louder he got. "Man, you know I don't like it when you guys touch my stuff! And what's that spoon in it for!"

"Excuse me," I said to Vanessa, as I slid through the cracked opening into the hall, closing the door behind me. "Why are you making a big fuss, man?"

"'Cause I got some folks coming over. Who's in there with you?"

"Uh, don't worry about it."

"Luckily I stopped at the Liquor Bank to get some more champagne and stuff. Whose car is that out front? It looks familiar."

"Why you gotta ask so many questions? Just go handle *your* business."

"Yeah, yeah, yeah." Dab retreated back down the stairs. "Just keep your paws off my stuff."

"Like you've never touched anybody else's stuff," I reminded him as I went back into my room. I knew that was just an excuse. The real reason he had come upstairs was to try to see who was with me. Dab was always trying to be slick.

"Where were we?" I asked, taking my seat next to Vanessa. I sat a little closer this time.

"I was telling you how intrigued I was." This time her soft hand reached for my face to draw it near. There was another hard knock on my door.

"Davey!" It was Doc. "Dab said we need those party music tapes you made."

"Give me a break!" I said to no one in particular. I went to my stereo cabinet and grabbed two cassettes. I handed them to Doc through the crack I opened in the door. "Here, man. What happened to L'il J's? Thought you guys were going there?"

"Change of plans-ski," he said. "We're doing an impromptu birthday party for Sheila here." He went back down the stairs.

I closed the door. This time I went over to my king-sized bed and sat on the edge. "Why don't you come over here?" I requested.

Vanessa stood up slowly and walked over to stand directly in front of me, between my spread legs. "I heard that you have a talented mouth," she breathed huskily.

I reached out for her small waist and pulled her closer. My hands slid down over her plump butt to the bottom of her dress, and then back up her smooth thighs under the dress, raising it slowly as my hands headed for the waistband of her thongs. There was a soft knock at the door.

"Davey?"

Renee!

Renee, the girl I've been seeing for a couple of months!!

Renee, plan B, supposed to be at home, waiting for me!!!

Renee—hot-tempered Renee!!!!

"Oh shit!" I exclaimed. Luckily, I had locked the door. I heard her tying the doorknob.

"What?" Vanessa asked.

"It's, uh … it's the girl I've been seeing," I explained.

"Oh." She remained calm, unlike someone else in that room. "What do you want me to do?"

"Davey?" Renee called again sweetly, "Get up and open the door, honey."

"Uh, uh, uh, *hide!*" I whispered to Vanessa. "One minute, baby," I called out—with a fake yawn—to the door.

"Hide?" Vanessa said, a little annoyed now. "I don't *think* so."

"For me. Do it for me. This girl has a bad temper. She's very, very jealous."

"She'll understand."

"Daaaaavvvvvvveeeeeeyyyyyyyyy!" she called with a little more insistence in her voice.

"Would you understand?"

"Yeah! Uh, well, maybe not, but I'm not hiding. Uh-uh. No way."

Then it hit me. "Go into the bathroom. It's a Jack-and-Jill. Go through and come out into Doc's bedroom and then go through his door out to the hallway and on downstairs where everyone else is."

"You owe me," she said, and then she ran her finger between her legs and put it up to my lips. It was wet and smelled *good*. I licked it and tried to put my hand between her legs. She backed away, shook her head with a smile, grabbed her purse, and headed into the bathroom.

"*Davey*, open the door!" insisted Renee, knocking harder as she twisted the doorknob.

I took off my shirt, kicked off my shoes, unbuckled my belt, and pulled back the comforter, and then went to open the door. I flung it open wide.

"Hey, baby," I said groggily, as I reached out to hug Renee. Over her shoulder, I saw Dab and Beverly coming up the stairs, just as the door to Doc's bedroom on the other side of the stairs opened and Vanessa stepped out into the hallway.

"Vanessa!" Beverly yelled. "I didn't know you were here!"

Dab's head jerked from Vanessa to me.

Vanessa looked at me.

Beverly turned toward me, saying "Oops."

And Renee stood in front of me with hands on hips, staring at me.

There was a long silence. It probably lasted a second, but it felt like forever.

"Uh, c'mon now," I blurted out, "you guys are going to, uh, spoil the surprise party! Sheila will be here, uh, any minute now. Go, uh, go back and hide, Vanessa! Dab! Beverly!"

No one moved. There was another moment of silence, and then the three of them looked at each other and just burst out laughing— all of them except Renee.

In fact, she didn't laugh all weekend. And I didn't get any from her that whole weekend either. But she cooled off after a few days, and then the make-up sex was extra nice Wednesday night.

Yep, Wednesday night, the night that Vanessa and the Ebony Fashion Fair finally left town for Oakland.

TOO MANY CHOICES

YOU KNOW, SOMETIMES THINGS JUST DON'T GO THE WAY YOU PLAN and it's a good thing—sometimes.

I went to First Fridays in Redondo Beach one Friday night just to do some work, which is the excuse I gave Evelyn, the latest honey in my life. I had been seeing her for a few months and, consequently, spending all my Friday evenings with her. At least that's how we started off.

You see, as mentioned, some ladies believe that if they are in a relationship, the guy is *supposed* to spend Friday and Saturday nights with her, especially when the relationship is new.

Yeah, right!

Anyway, being the nice guy that I was—at the time—I adhered to her way of thinking. *BIG* mistake. Buying into a woman's way of thinking means *you* are not thinking. It lets *her* think that she has you under control, which is the last thing you should let a woman think unless you are a fool or in love.

Anyway, I told myself that I was neither. You see, in a relationship—especially a new relationship—you're either the trainer or the trainee. So I had to break her out of the idea of us being together *every* Friday. I was *not* going to be the trainee. However, I did tell her that I would be over after I got done "working." Hey, the girl had some good pussy.

Back in those daze—yep, *daze*—"good pussy" was a redundant

statement to me. You see, I used to have this saying: "The worst pussy I ever had was good; the fact that it's pussy makes it good."

Now, Evelyn was a catch, all right. She was fine and had a great body, a good job, no kids, and an ex-husband. She lived alone, could cook, and drove a nice car. And did I mention that she had some *good* pussy? What more can you want in a lady? Before you answer that, let me ask another question. Why does the grass always seem greener on the other side, no matter which side you're on? That's right; both questions are rhetorical.

At any rate, I hadn't been to a First Fridays event since I started seeing Evelyn. These events were hosted by a group of ladies who were friends of ours. They did these happy hour affairs on the first Friday of every month at various venues in and around Los Angeles, hence the name. They always started at six o'clock and ended at midnight. The functions were considered networking affairs. All you had to do was make sure your "net" was working.

Usually the attendees were a nice group of professional Black people in the LA basin. And the female attendees were a wonderful sight to behold. However, I knew that Evelyn was the only one I was supposed to be holding this night.

The reason I was "out to work" was that the fellas—Dab, Doug, and Doc—had recently started promoting a Friday-night soiree at a new club in Beverly Hills called Rendezvous with some other promoters. I had invested money in the promotion at the outset, so I, Davey Stein, was extended a partnership. Plus we were all roommates and were known as the 4Ds for a while, but Doug was getting married soon, so we were going to be the new 3Ds.

We were part of the in-crowd. Folks knew or had heard of us because of the parties we'd given at the Mini-Mansion and the various nightclubs we'd been involved with through the years.

Okay, that was a commercial break. Now, back to this night.

We had some colorful five-by-seven glossy flyers printed up, plus some VIP cards, and tonight we were in the streets passing them out. We were *working* the streets, going to various happy hour spots to promote our spot.

Dab and Doc had a few other happy hours that they were going to hit first in other parts of the city to recruit, and then they were going to meet me at First Fridays, which we considered the prime place to do our recruiting of new ladies this week. And, of course, *new ladies* were always our objective.

From there we were going to head on over to Rendezvous hopefully, with quite a few of the attendees in tow, especially the females—the best-looking females, the CODs—with VIP cards in hand.

I arrived at the Redondo Beach Bay Club in the city's marina harbor around seven o'clock. This was my favorite of the various venues that the First Fridays group used. For some reason, the turnout was always a little better when they held their affairs in the beach cities: Redondo Beach, Manhattan Beach, Venice Beach, Santa Monica, and Marina del Rey. I guess the cuties had an affinity for the Pacific Ocean. And I understood. There was something about the smell of the ocean that made me feel more alive—or was that more horny? That intoxicating ocean air ...

They were out in droves this night, I noticed, as I saw groups of CODs walking toward the entrance.

I always found parking myself instead of letting the valets park my ride. Now, if I'd had a new Mercedes or BMW or some other fancy car, I would've let them handle it so the cuties could see me roll up. But I hadn't gotten my black Lincoln LS yet. I was still in my old diesel Mercedes, which had a glitch. I had to raise the hood to stop the engine from running when I turned off the ignition. I parked it, and since I didn't want anyone to see me under the hood, I waited for folks to pass on by before I turned it off.

Unexpectedly, two cuties were walking by, heading toward the club as I was letting my hood down.

"Is everything all right?" one of them asked. There's nothing like a concerned Black woman. That usually means that she's the nurturing type.

"Uh, yeah, yeah," I quickly lied. "I was just, uh, checking, uh, my battery."

"Okay," she said as they kept on by.

I headed toward the club behind them, checking them out. Both were very attractive. The one who had spoken, however, was a nine on a scale of one to ten—maybe a nine and a half. She had on an orange-and-yellow summer dress that showed a pair of great legs and couldn't hide a booty that moved graciously with every step. Her buddy in blue was more like a seven.

I'm a butt man. That is my favorite part of the female anatomy. Most of the fellas are into big breasts—I called them "baby dinners," and I've always said, "If it's mo' than a mouthful, it's a waste."

Booties are my thing. Something happens inside of me when I see a nice butt. My adrenaline starts bubbling.

Now, when I say "nice" butt, I don't mean a big, way-out-of-proportion butt. I mean a butt that's round and plump yet firm, and attached to a body from five feet six to five feet nine, weighing between 120 and 135, depending on the height—a booty just a little this side of *"Dayum!"*

I took a deep breath of the ocean air as I quickened my pace to catch up to the two ladies while pulling some of the flyers out of the inside pocket of my sport coat.

"Excuse me, ladies."

They slowed down and turned to me.

"Yes?" the girl in the blue dress inquired.

I fell into pace with them. "In case you guys are interested in going someplace else tonight when this is over"—I handed each a flyer—"my buddies and I have this new spot called Rendezvous on LaCienega in Beverly Hills. You ought to check us out tonight."

"This is the spot I was telling you about earlier," Blue Dress said to her friend.

"And what did you tell her?" asked I.

"That I was there last Friday and liked it."

"Uh huh, that's what she told me," her friend confirmed. "And who are you?"

By this time, we had reached the entrance.

"Hey, Davey, how you doing?" One of the First Fridays hostesses was standing at the entrance, conversing with one of the hired security workers.

"Hey, Tracey," I responded.

"What's up, Davey?" greeted the guy working security at the door.

"Hey, Robert," I returned. He sometimes worked the door at our club too.

"Are they with you?" Tracey asked, indicating the two cuties.

"Uh, yep," I fibbed.

Tracey held up three fingers to two of her cohorts at the table just inside the entrance, and they gave her three wristbands, which she handed to me. "Enjoy yourselves. Ladies, please sign our guest book if you haven't already done so. Davey, we'll probably see you later tonight at your spot."

"Bet," I acknowledged. "The fellas are on their way over here too."

"Oh, I got Doc and Dab covered," replied Tracey.

That's what I like about the Black nightclub scene in LA; the promoters all have each other's backs. If you're a nightclub promoter, you get love when you go to a fellow promoter's spot; and said promoter gets love when he or she comes to your spot. It's an unwritten law between most folks who run clubs in LA.

"Thanks for getting us in free, Davey," the girl in orange and yellow said after they signed the book and we proceeded inside. "My name is Honore, and this is Debra."

"No problem." I shrugged. "Perhaps I'll see you guys later tonight at my spot. Here's a VIP card."

"Thanks. You probably will," Honore said as a group of squealing girls swooped down on them. "We're celebrating a birthday here tonight. See you later, and thanks again." The girls whisked them away to the back section of the club.

I turned and saw a nice booty at the bar and decided I needed a drink. The booty was attached to a short, sexy cutie in a form-fitting purple dress. It was like a magnet pulling me over to the bar.

"Cuba libre with Myers's rum, tall, with a splash of Rose's lime juice," I ordered as I reached the booty, fighting the urge to let the back of my hand brush against it "accidentally."

"Cuba libre? What's that?" the booty babe asked.

I turned to look into some dark brown eyes with long, curled lashes. The purple dress had a V-shaped neckline that dipped just enough to show her cleavage and the inner halves of her twins. They looked to be identical.

"It's a rum and Coke," I replied, "but when you add a lime wedge or lime juice to a rum and Coke, it becomes a cuba libre, and I like my rum to be Myers's."

"Oh, okay," she accepted. "I think I know you."

"You do?" I grinned.

"Yeah, don't you live in that house they call the Mini-Mansion on Olympiad?"

"Uh, yeah."

"I came to a party there with some friends before. You live there with this brother who looks like one of the Whispers and a doctor and a photographer. Right?"

"Yeah, that's us, but the photographer is moving out; he's getting married."

"What's your name?"

"I'm Davey." I chuckled. She seemed a little aggressive, but her booty—I mean beauty—made me overlook that. "What's yours?"

"I'm Ronnie," she acknowledged, sticking out her hand.

I shook her hand. It was soft, but she had a strong grip. I like that in a woman. The deejay struck up a popular dance tune.

"Wanna dance?" Ronnie asked.

I'm not that much of an up-tempo tune dancer. I prefer dancing slow and close. But I decided to accept her offer. We left our drinks at the bar, and I followed her to the dance area.

Walking behind her was mesmerizing. Her ass was just a little bigger than what I called the perfect butt. The perfect butt belonged to a model named Joi Ryda, whom I had seen in photos a while back. Ronnie's was close. She walked as if she wanted men to look at her, with her cheeks moving from side to side with each step, like two

basketballs in a sack saying, "Yo' turn, my turn, yo' turn, my turn."
And in between steps, they trembled, awaiting the next step.

We danced to two consecutive songs. Her booty bumped into
me accidentally a few times—at least I thought they were accidents.

I followed her derriere back to our drinks.

"That was fun," she said, taking a swallow. "You come to these
functions a lot?"

"I try to. These girls are friends of ours, so we try to support
them, as they do us."

I told her about Rendezvous and gave her a couple of flyers. I
was ready to continue circulating. I've never been one to lock onto
one lady when I go to clubs or to a party. One of my roomies, Doc
Holliday, tended to spot a lady he liked when we first got to an affair
and spend the entire evening talking to that one lady. And then later
he would complain that the lady kept him from getting to other
cuties he saw.

Not me. When I was out, I was out to work my net. If I saw
someone I liked, I'd speak to her off and on throughout the evening,
and if I thought there's some interest, I'd ask for her number or give
her mine, and we'd talk at length later. I was just not one to latch on
to one lady all night when there were so many more around that I
could attend to. Some ladies seem to think a guy is a dog when he
does that. To me it's just about being social, networking, and keeping
your options open.

Now, I'm not saying that I'm all that. I mean, ladies seem to
like my eyes and smile. I don't see it, but they do, and that's all that
matters to me.

I discreetly excused myself from Ronnie and her prying questions
under the pretense of going to the men's room. When I emerged from
there, I went in the opposite direction, away from her, to get a look
at the crowd, handing out flyers to folks, concentrating more on
good-looking ladies and slipping some—the best-looking ones—VIP
cards.

After I had been there a couple of hours, Dab and Doc showed
up. Dab happened to see Honore when she walked by to go to the

ladies' room and was smitten. We were standing by the middle bar, getting drinks.

"Now, that's nice there," he said in admiration.

"Yeah, I met her when I first got here," I said. "She and some of her girls are coming by Rendezvous later."

"So are you talking to her?" Dab asked.

I knew that meant he wanted to move on her.

"She's in the running," I admitted. "You know I like to bide my time."

"Don't bide your time too long with Dab-ski on the prowl-ski," Doc cautioned, with a chuckle.

"Who told you," I said.

Dab and I were constantly bumping heads when it came to the ladies. Although he was several inches shorter than I, at five ten—which he called six feet—we basically liked the same style of ladies: very attractive ladies from five six to five nine. The only difference was that he preferred them slender and light-skinned and didn't care whether they had nice booties or not. That's why some of his conquests were White girls. I didn't care how light or dark they were, but they *had to* have nice booties. That's why I very rarely hit on White girls.

"Wait until you see the one we saw over at Joseph's," Dab said, "Tell him, Holliday."

"Aw, man," Doc responded, "her and her three girlfriends looked like Destiny's Child. I just hope they show up."

"They'll show," predicted Dab. "I gave them VIP cards and told them their drinks are on me."

"They'll show!" Doc and I agreed in unison.

We passed out flyers to most of the good-looking ladies there as we chatted with them and their friends, even though some of the ladies we targeted didn't have cute friends. We had to bite the bullet on those.

When ladies are in a group, you can't invite just the good-looking ones. Not all good-looking females have—or travel with—good-looking friends. And sometimes the unattractive members of groups control where they do or do not go. We had to be very diplomatic in those situations. Sometimes we even had to approach an unattractive one first just to get her in our corner in an attempt to defuse any cock-blocking action.

And, of course, we passed out flyers to the cool brothers in the place too. These guys were assets to a club's success. Cool brothers usually drank the cool drinks—cognac, brandy, vodka, champagne—and bought drinks for the ladies. And ladies like to have drinks sent to them by good-looking cool brothers. It kept them coming back.

We decided it was time to get on over to Rendezvous. Dab talked me into leaving my car in the parking lot there at the bay club. He wanted to show off his new black-on-black Mercedes that he'd just bought. He and Doc had been rolling in it all afternoon, even before going to the happy hours. Dab's apparel business was doing well.

Just as the valet pulled up with Dab's ride, a red BMW rolled up and a beauty got out dressed in red from head to toe; she even had a red ribbon in her hair. She was light, bright, and damn-near White, with long, flowing sandy hair, pert breasts, and a nice, delicious apple.

Dab was busy tipping the valet, but I saw his eyes get big. "Give that lady an invitation, Holliday!" he hollered out to Doc, who was lagging behind him.

"An invitation to what?" the COD asked, displaying a lovely flirtatious smile, looking at the black Mercedes.

"To our club tonight," I said, beating Doc over to her.

"And what club is that?"

"Rendezvous, over on LaCienega, across the street from the Gate," I told her.

"Oh, I was gonna go there tonight," she cooed, walking toward Dab's car with me.

"The Gate or Rendezvous?" asked I.

"Rendezvous," she replied. "The Gate is a little too rowdy for me; there's always a commotion going on over there."

"Here's a VIP card. You won't have to stand in a long line at our spot."

"Why, thank you." She smiled, accepting the card. "My name is Cherry."

The valets were pulling up other cars behind us, giving Dab the eye because he was slowing things down.

"We gotta roll, man," Dab said, getting in the car.

"That's Dab," I introduced quickly, indicating him in the car. "I'm Davey, and that's Joseph," I nodded in Doc's direction as he slid into the front seat.

"Hi!" he called out.

"We're holding up these other cars, Cherry Red," I explained, getting in the backseat.

"No problem," the red-clad cutie said, "I'll look for you when I get there."

We pulled off.

"That's one bad mama," Doc said. "Which one of you guys going for her?"

"She's fair game," I answered. "Right, Dab?"

"They're all fair game," responded Dab. "Women do the real choosing. We just think it's on us."

"Doug-ski finally got through to you, huh?" Doc laughed.

"I always knew that," Dab shot back. "Doug didn't have to tell me. Anyway, I'm playing it cool till the girl from Joseph's shows up."

"What's her name?" I inquired.

"Now, you know Dab-ski don't remember names." Doc chuckled.

"Her name is Sandi," Dab said.

"Damn!" exclaimed Doc. "I'm impressed."

"She must've been all that and more," I said, equally surprised.

It was almost ten o'clock when we reached Rendezvous. There was a long line waiting to get in. The VIP line was a lot shorter and moved quicker, because the folks just showed their cards, got VIP armbands, and went on inside. And sure enough, most of them were females—very attractive females. As Terrence Howard said in the movie *The Best Man*, it was going to be a "ho-asis" in the club tonight.

Our other four partners were waiting inside for us. We all

huddled in our roped-off private VIP booth on the first level, just off the dance floor. They filled us in on what had transpired before we arrived.

Stewart Stone handled the dinner portion of the early evening, which featured a jazz artist. Sterling Sutton had arranged a private party for one of his friends on the city council up in the VIP room. It was over now, but most of his invitees were mingling throughout the club, and the VIP room was now open to all with the VIP armbands. Ronaldo Wood had a popular recording star coming in to play some cuts from her soon-to-be released CD. Richard Butts had a group of his entertainment industry and pro athlete friends making appearances to add some flavor. The four of them said folks had already been showing up flashing the flyers that Doc, Dab, and I had handed out earlier. We expected a hell of a crowd.

The only thing for us to do now was to roam the club and make sure everything was running smoothly. We took turns at the front door, checking tickets after the patrons paid at the window outside. We kept an eye on the back door out in the patio area to make sure folks were not trying to sneak in. We also made trips to the restroom to make sure no drugs were being done. We had security roaming also, but we liked keeping our fingers on the pulse for that personal touch.

We also checked with the deejay, the waitresses, and the bartenders on the main floor and up in the VIP room from time to time to make sure they didn't need anything or have a customer with a complaint. Other than that, we were there to enjoy the ladies too. I know I was.

You see, running a nightclub wasn't just about making money. And, yeah, there was money to be made. It was about good customer service, keeping the spot popular and popping. But it was also about doing something that was fun to do and meeting some bad ladies in the process.

Ladies gravitate to guys who run nightclubs. I discovered that long ago. They know that you can do favors for them, such as letting them in free, not making them stand in line, sending free drinks over, giving them access to the VIP area, and generally allowing them to look good among their friends. And these women have a nice way of showing their appreciation for such favors. Hell, if they didn't show their appreciation occasionally, they'd stop getting the favors.

"Hey, Davey." One of the blonde waitresses approached me as I was out on the patio, talking to the photographer our other partner, Doug, had hired. "Stew wants to see you at the front door."

"All right," I said.

"There's a lady outside asking for you," Stew told me when I reached the front. He opened the door and had security send her in. It was Ronnie, with the nice booty draped in purple, from the First Fridays event. Stew directed her to me.

"Hi again." She smiled apprehensively when she saw my frown.

"Hi back at ya," I said. "What's up?"

"I thought I was your guest tonight."

I started to say, "What made you think that?" I intentionally hadn't given her a VIP card. I had just given her a flyer. I decided not to embarrass her by mentioning that. *Hell, I might need a "favor" later. And she does have that banging body, although she's a little shorter than I like.*

"Well, you're in now," I said, nodding okay to Stew. "You been here before?"

"No," she replied. "This is my first time."

"Well, hang out and enjoy yourself." I turned and walked away, knowing I'd hear from her during the evening.

The way we'd done things in the past was to invite the ladies we were hitting on to the private VIP booth, which was guarded by one of our security personnel. We had a VIP room upstairs that folks who had the VIP armbands could go to. But for anyone other than us to sit at our VIP booth on the main floor, the security had to hear our code word, which we changed every Friday.

Our earlier "work" was paying off; the honeys were pouring into Rendezvous. The VIP room upstairs was stocked with CODs. And since everything was running effortlessly, I decided it was time to see whether I wanted to have breakfast with one of these cuties on duty before I hooked up with Evelyn.

I went up to the VIP room. Dab and Doc were already there. Dab was talking to a lady at the bar who looked a lot like Beyoncé. I figured it had to be Sandi, the girl he and Doc had been bragging about in the car. I went over to them.

"What's up, Dab?" I said, looking at the beauty.

"Davey, this is Sandi. Sandi, this is another one of my partners, and roommate, Davey."

The long-lashed lovely smiled. "So you're the one, huh?"

"What one?" I asked, playing along.

"The playboy extraordinaire," she said with a smile.

"Me?"

"That's what yo' boys here say," she shared.

"They're just covering their own asses," I informed her. "They're the dogs; I'm just a puppy in training."

"Being a playa is not being a dog," enlightened Sandi. "Dogs can kiss my ass. A playa? Hell, I might kiss his."

"In that case, I *am* a playa," I joked.

"Tell it, girl," another cutie said, walking up to us with Doc.

"This is Davey, the playboy of the group," Sandi introduced. "This is my ace, Tanzy."

"Hi, Tanzy," I greeted. "But again, these guys are bigger playas than I am."

"Yeah, right," Dab and Doc said together.

"Sandi, Tanzy, don't be fooled," I warned. Just then I saw Honore enter the VIP room from the back stairs "Excuse me." I left them.

"There goes the playa-ski," Doc said. They all laughed.

"Hey you." I approached Honore. *Wow, she is looking good*, I noted.

She smiled. "There you are."

"You're looking good, girl."

"Thank you. You're not bad either."

"What are you drinking?"

"An apple martini would be nice."

"You got it."

We hung upstairs together for almost an hour, after which she left to touch base with her crew. I told her to meet me at our VIP booth later. I gave her the code word for the night. I headed down the front steps above the entrance a few minutes after Honore went down the back steps near the bar. A beauty in red was coming up as I was heading down. It was Cherry.

"Hey there," I said.

"Hi." She smiled. "Davey, right?"

"Who told you."

"You did."

I chuckled. "No, that 'who told you' means 'you got that right.'"

"Ooo-kay! Where're your friends?"

"They're up there."

"C'mon back up with me," she requested.

I turned and followed her shapely booty back up the stairs.

The fellas were where I had left them, still talking to Sandi and Tanzy.

"He got another one," I heard Sandi say out of the corner of her mouth. They all laughed.

I did the honors. "Cherry, this is Sandi and Tanzy. You've met the fellas."

"What are you drinking?" Dab asked.

"Why, champagne, of course," she declared, looking at the flutes they all had.

Sandi smiled. "Our kind of girl." They all were feeling good, it seemed.

I saw Doc indicate for me to look behind me. I did and saw Evelyn making a beeline toward me. This was the girl that I'd been seeing for a few months—the girl who was supposed to be at home waiting for me. *What's wrong with these ladies?* I mused as I moved toward her before she reached us.

"Hey, honey." She hugged me, kissing me on the cheek. "I know you're busy. What's the code word for the VIP booth? I got Annette waiting for me downstairs." I whispered it in her ear. "Okay, I'll see you downstairs later."

Damn! I thought. *Why do these ladies have to be so hardheaded? She's supposed to be at home, waiting on me to call her. Now she and Honore are both waiting for me at the booth.*

"Ain't she supposed to be at home-ski waiting for you to call her?" Doc asked, walking up.

"Who told you."

"Where's yo' champagne?" Cherry inquired, looking at my empty hands when Doc and I returned to their cluster. Sandi didn't miss anything, it seemed, she was grinning knowingly at me.

I definitely need a drink now, I thought as I got a flute from the bartender. Dab poured the bubbly into my glass from the bottle he was holding.

"A toast," proposed Cherry, hooking her arm with mine. We raised our glasses. "May all our pain be champagne."

I stayed upstairs long enough to finish my drink, hear Dab mention breakfast at the house or at Berrie's—a late-night eatery over on Third—and have a slow dance with Cherry. Her soft body molded into mine. She caused some rambunctious behavior in the front of my slacks.

I roamed the club, hanging out mostly at the front door, trying to stay away from the VIP booth for as long as I could. I was hoping to see Honore away from the booth, away from Evelyn, so I could have some private words with her. She was the one I wanted to be with the most. No such luck.

Last call was announced.

"They're looking for you at the booth, Cuba Libre," Richard Butts told me when he stepped outside and saw me chatting with some of the security staff. He liked calling me by my favorite drink's name.

"They who?" I asked.

"The fellas ... and the girls." He laughed. I took a deep breath and followed him over to our VIP booth.

Time to face the music, I thought.

When I got there, I saw Dab, Doc, Ronaldo, and Sterling with

Sandi, Tanzy, Cherry, Honore, Honore's friend Debra, Evelyn, Annette, and Ronnie. Richard took his seat at the end around the big table. They squeezed in to make room for me at the other end, but I grabbed an empty chair from a nearby table and sat in it instead.

I looked at Honore. She smiled.

I looked at Evelyn. She smiled and winked.

I looked at Cherry. She winked.

Ronnie was looking at me seductively.

Sandi was grinning at me; that girl didn't miss anything. "You need a drink, don't you, Extraordinaire?" she asked, sitting next to Dab.

"Who told you," I said rhetorically.

"I decided to fix breakfast for everyone at the house," Dab announced to me, "instead of going to Berrie's." He loved to cook for groups of folks, especially if females were involved. He used his cooking to impress them, since he really was a good cook. Many had heard about his culinary skills; his gumbo was legendary, and he made some great omelets, along with his many other dishes. He usually prepared the food for all our house parties.

"Oh, yeah?" I replied, accepting the flute of champagne that was passed around to me. "Who all's coming?"

"Everyone here," Richard answered, smirking. "The question is, are *you*?"

"Very funny, man," I replied, kicking him lightly. He laughed.

"We all are hungry, baby," Evelyn informed me from across the table.

Now, whose benefit was that "baby" for? I thought.

I didn't know how this situation was going to play out. The evening had started with me planning on hooking up with Evelyn. It could still end that way. But I thought, *Do I want that now?* I had been seeing her for a few months, but she wasn't my girlfriend. We had no labels. Now, Cherry got my dander up. Ronnie had been giving strong availability signs from the get-go. Honore had lots of potential and seemed the classiest. Class was a *big* turn-on to me.

It was time. 2:00 a.m. was club-closing time in LA. That law was one of the things I disliked about Los Angeles. I mean, there were after-hours clubs in the inner city, but some of those were risky places to go to. For the most part, after the clubs closed one could go to a house party one had heard about or to a twenty-four-hour restaurant and not be at risk.

"Uh, Dab, remember you have to take me to my car," I reminded him.

"I can take you," offered Evelyn.

"No," Dab objected, "I might as well do it. I gotta stop at a supermarket anyway. Holliday, why don't you ride with Rich and open the house for everyone and keep them happy till we get there."

"No problem-ski," Doc concurred. "And I have our shares from tonight already." He passed out envelopes to the fellas.

Everyone stood up. Evelyn came up to say that they were going to hurry outside to beat the long line for the valet and that she would see me when I got to the house. She hugged me and left with Annette. Holliday organized the ones who hadn't been to the Mini-Mansion before to tell them to caravan behind him in Rich's gray Mercedes. I went up to Honore to tell her not to get lost.

She smiled wanly.

"Let's hit it, man," Dab said.

We left the club. Dab got his keys from the valet, and we went to the parking lot behind the club to retrieve his car. He drove out the back way through the alley to avoid the valet rush up front. A half hour later, we were in the parking lot of the Redondo Beach Bay Club, in front of my car.

"Okay, man," I said, getting out, "I'll see you back at the house."

Dab grinned. "Yeah, I'm looking forward to that. I want to see your balancing act with three ladies."

"Four," I corrected.

"Four?"

"Yeah, that crazy Ronnie chick."

"You're in trouble, man. I gotta make sure to get some popcorn." He was laughing as he drove off.

I'm not looking forward to it, I thought as I got in my car and turned the key. Nothing happened. *What the!* I tried the key again. Nothing. Just a click. *I don't believe this shit!* I thought. I turned on the lights. No good. *It's the battery,* I deduced. I got out of the car to raise the hood. I didn't know if the battery was bad or if it was corrosion on the cables. The cables looked good. I deducted that I needed a jump.

"Is everything all right?"

Déjà vu, I thought. *I'm reliving hearing a voice asking that same question several hours earlier.*

"Davey, is everything all right?"

I jerked around, surprised to hear my name. It was Honore and Debra. I'd been so engrossed with looking under the hood that I hadn't heard them drive up.

"No, everything is not all right. It won't start."

"Debbie, you go ahead on; I'll call you tomorrow," Honore said, getting out of the car.

"Okay, girl," Debra responded. "You know I gotta go see about my baby. See you later." And with that, she was gone.

"So, mister," Honore said, standing beside me, "you're having car trouble, huh? Is it the battery?"

"Exactly."

"Do you have cables?"

"Yeah, I do."

"Okay, let me get my car."

She drove her car over close to mine. We hooked up the cables. We stood there and talked as the vehicles connected for a while to get my battery a little stronger.

"Thank you, lady."

"You're lucky I left my car here too, sir."

"So does this mean that you were not coming by the house for breakfast?"

"Yes, that's what it means. You seem to have your hands full tonight."

"It would seem that way," I admitted, "but, quiet as it's kept, my hands prefer you—and that's no lie."

"Is that right?"

"That's right."

"Hmmmmm."

"In fact, it seems that Fate decided that she wants us to hook up like these two cars."

"So Fate arranged for us to meet like this?"

"Yeah, it's not just a coincidence. It was meant to be."

"You think so?"

"Uh-huh. So what were you planning on doing now?"

"Go home."

"Someone waiting for you there?"

"No, but I know someone is waiting for *you*."

"Aren't you hungry?"

"Yes, I am, but I'm surely not going to your place."

"Well, let's you and I go have breakfast somewhere out here."

"What about the folks at your house?"

"I'm sure they'll have fun without me."

"Hmm, I'm willing to bet it's more fun *with* you. That's why that one lady let it be known?"

"What one lady?"

"You know who I'm talking about. I think her name was Evelyn?"

"Well, she's a friend."

"Davey, I'm no dummy; that woman was acting like more than a friend."

"I've known her for a few months. We go out sometimes, but we have no labels."

"She seems like she *wants* a label."

"Well, I don't."

"Why not?"

"Because I'm not feeling her like that."

"And I'm supposed to believe that, right?"

"Yes, believe that, because it's true. I'm interested in getting to know *you*."

"And why's that?"

"'Cause I *am* feeling *you*."

"You're feeling me, huh?"

"Yeah, I'm feeling you. I want to get to know you."

"What you want to know about me?"

"Are you really as nice as you appear?"

"And?"

"Are you really as classy, as caring, as friendly, as—"

"Okay, okay." Honore laughed. "I think maybe we ought to go to breakfast so I can answer those questions."

"Now, why didn't I think of that?" I smiled as I opened the door on the passenger side to let her into my car.

"Okay, I'll take a chance in *your* car," she chuckled.

I laughed as we headed to the nearest restaurant.

Yep, sometimes things don't go the way you planned. And sometimes that's a *good* thing.

GOOD AT BEING BADD

(An Erotic Interlude)

WE HAVE QUITE A FEW NICE MALLS IN THE CITY OF ANGELS. WE have the Beverly Center, the Crenshaw Mall, Century City, Westside Pavilion, and the South Bay Mall. We even have a mall-like spot called the Grove that just sprang up, and a spot called the Bridge. But if you asked a Black man which mall he would go to if he wanted to see some fine "angels," he'd tell you he'd go to the Fox Hills Mall.

Fox Hills is an area just off Slauson, west of LaCienega, not far from the Mini-Mansion. The area consists of apartment complexes, condos, a park, several hotels, and some of the best-looking chicks in LA.

I guess after they heard the name of the area, the "foxes" decided they *had to* live in those "Hills." The mall was right on the edge of it, so the foxes flocked to it, as did the females from View Park, Baldwin Hills, Ladera Heights, Culver City, Inglewood, Marina del Rey, and all over the southwest LA vicinity—and, consequently, so did the wolves.

I liked going there alone sometimes on a Saturday afternoon to just girl-watch up in the food court area or browse the department stores—especially their fragrance departments. You can find some good stuff around the cosmetics area of a store when you're on the prowl—customers *and* employees. The scent of prey was overwhelming.

I was just stepping out into the mall from the May Company when I picked up the scent of Issey Miyake, which was one of my favorite fragrances. I sniffed the air and attempted to follow the spoor. That's when I looked around and saw a beautiful fox window-shopping.

She had on a pleated white tennis skirt and a sleeveless pink T-shirt. She stood about five feet seven. She was an eye pleaser. There was something exotic about her appearance, with her long jet-black hair and dark eyes. Puerto Rico came to mind, or perhaps Bermuda, Cuba, or some other island. She was built like Jennifer Lopez but had a prettier face; and that's saying something, because J-Lo is very good looking to me. And of course she had that J-Lo booty. Uh, did you catch on that I'm a booty man?

For me, if the female body in question doesn't come with a great booty, then that's not the female body for me. I will not touch it. Won't lay a glove on it. That's my aphrodisiac. I don't need oysters or broccoli or pills. Just show me the booty!

Don't get me wrong. I'm not saying that I would knock off a mud duck if she had a nice booty. Oh no. I had standards. That booty had to have a pretty face topping that frame. It had to have a personality too. I'd deviated from those standards only once. And that girl— Bertha—had a body even better than the one belonging to this lady in the pleated skirt. And that's saying a lot, because this lady in front of me was B-A-double D! Badd! And that's good.

I discreetly watched the short white skirt stroll along, stopping in front of some of the shops on the first level and checking out the displays. I saw quite a few guys walking by, checking out *her* display. Some of them almost bumped into each other in the process. She seemed unaware of the folks around her.

I meandered behind her.

There was a Mexican restaurant that served some good margaritas nearby. She passed by it to gaze in the window of the shop next door. But just as I was reaching the restaurant, she suddenly doubled back to enter the eatery. Since I was right there, I opened the door, stepped back, and bade her to go on in.

"Thank you, kind sir." She smiled as she stepped through the opening.

"You're welcome, fine ma'am," I replied.

There was a slight trace of an accent, I noticed, as I got a whiff of her perfume when she passed by. Yep, she was the one wearing Issey Miyake. I also noticed her long nipples making an imprint against her top. Her smile was very friendly. She had deep dimples and some great DSLs, which is what the fellas and I called full, plump, juicy-looking dick-sucking lips. They weren't big lips, but they most definitely were not little either. They were soft, sensuous-looking lips.

I went on inside of the restaurant too. The scintillating lady sauntered over to the bar with one of the sexiest walks I'd ever seen, as if she were on a runway, modeling.

She was the Pied Piper. I followed.

"I'll have a strawberry margarita," I heard her say as she took a seat on the lone vacant barstool. There was a big space between her stool and the one next to her for the waitstaff to use, but there was room enough for me to sidle in there without getting in their way.

The bartender looked at me questioningly. "Uh, put her drink on my tab, and I'll have a Cadillac margarita on the rocks, no salt," I ordered, foregoing my usual cuba libre.

"Oh, my gentleman friend, thank you," the cutie acknowledged, looking at me.

I chuckled. "I'm not a friend yet, but I'll fill out an application."

"That's cute." She laughed. Even her laughter had an exotic, sexy flavor about it.

"Are you from here?" I asked.

"No," she replied. "You?"

"Yes, born and raised in sunny, tropical Southern California," I said. "Where are you from?"

"Rio de Janeiro."

"I should have known."

"Why you say?"

"Because you're the best-looking thing in this whole mall."

"I bet you say to all."

"I wouldn't say that to Halle Berry, Beyoncé, Ciara, Claudia Jordan, Meagan Good, Meagan Badd ..."

"You funny." She laughed.

"How long you been here?"

"Two years. I come to be star. I second runner-up in Miss Brazil contest before."

"*Second* runner-up? Damn, the two in front of you would probably give me a heart attack!"

"You funny. They are beautiful girls. My good friends. They come soon."

"Come soon? Here! To the mall?"

She laughed. "No, no, no. Here to Los Angeles."

"Whew! Don't scare me, girl. I couldn't handle three beautiful, sexy ladies at once."

"I think you handle."

"Why?"

"Your eyes. Your eyes tell me you handle."

"I can handle you. What's your name?"

"Alana."

"Alana, I'm Davey."

"Baby?"

"No, Day-vee."

"I might want to call you Bay-bee."

"You can call me whatever you want, as long as you call me."

She laughed.

"You have a boyfriend?" I asked.

"I have friends. Don't like boys."

"Oh, you like girls?"

She laughed her exotic laugh again. "I like man. You man, Bay-bee?"

"I man, baby, I definitely man."

"I believe; I definitely believe. You *good* man?"

"When I'm good, I'm very good; but when I'm bad, I'm better."

She laughed. "Whooooo, you scare me."

"Don't want to scare you."

"No, no, I like; I like scare."

We sat there and talked for about an hour, drinking margaritas. I ordered some appetizers for us. In the process, I learned that she worked as an extra on television shows, movies, and commercials through a casting agency, and that she was taking classes at the fashion institute downtown. She also shared that her aunt owned a small gift shop in Manhattan Beach, and she helped her run it. I also learned that she was twenty-five years old and a Scorpio.

"You know 'bout Scorpio, eh?" she asked with a smile, working on her third drink. We snacked on some nachos and mini tacos to soak up the margaritas.

"I know what they say."

"Alana bad girl they say."

"Bad is good."

"Uh, when good, very good; when bad, better?"

I laughed. "Yeah, you got it."

"I got it. You want it?"

"Who told you," I replied.

Just sitting there with her for that hour was intoxicating. Her scent; her brown nipples, which I spied while looking down her top when she bent over to laugh; her long, soft, wavy hair; her caramel eyes; the sensuous way her butt moved when she went to the ladies' room—everything about her was turning me all the way on. I didn't want to part company with her.

"I have to go to aunt's shop."

"Oh no," I said.

"You follow?" she asked, her hand resting on my thigh.

"Huh?"

"You follow," she stated, looking into my eyes as she slightly squeezed my thigh.

"Uh, okay."

Manhattan Beach was a beach community just south of LAX. The streets closest to the beach had apartments, condos, duplexes, some small houses, balloon shops, boutiques, gift shops, bars, restaurants, and bicycle and skate rental shops. A lot of these buildings and shops a few blocks from the ocean were close together. Of course, palm trees were everywhere.

It took us over a half hour to get there. It should've taken twenty minutes. We parked in spaces in the carport.

"You always drive so slowly?" I asked her as we walked toward some stairs.

"I not want to lose you."

"You didn't have to worry about *that.*"

"I can't lose you?"

"No, you probably couldn't lose a blind man. As beautiful as you are, Stevie Wonder would've followed you, driving his own car."

"You funny man. You gentle man?"

"Yes, I consider myself a gentleman."

"No, no. You gentle?"

"Oh. Sometimes gentle, sometimes not too gentle."

She stopped and gave me a quick peck on the lips. "Good!" she said.

"No, no, no. Bad! Remember?"

She laughed.

I followed her up the stairs to a small gift shop. It was above a boutique on a narrow street, a couple of blocks from the beach. I could smell that intoxicating ocean air. I was getting an eyeful of her butt and pink thong peeking out of the bottom of her skirt as she ascended the steps.

She must have felt my eyes on her bottom, because when she reached the top of the stairs, she stopped abruptly before stepping to the door ahead. She wiggled her butt at me.

I was a couple of steps below her, but I extended my hand up to her soft thigh and slid up it to squeeze a cheek. She pushed her butt back toward me. I stepped up to her level and squeezed more, and then I wormed a finger around and under the crotch of her thong and encountered wetness. I slid that finger back and forth over her increasingly wet vagina lips as she whimpered and looked back at me. I then removed my hand, brought that finger to my mouth, and sucked her juice off it.

"Let's get inside," she said huskily, unlocking the door.

"That's where I want to be," said I, and I wasn't talking about the shop.

It was a small shop with shelves on the walls displaying mugs, T-shirts, caps, ashtrays, and cameras. There were racks holding more T-shirts, sunglasses, film, postcards, and miscellaneous souvenir items.

She went to the phone on the counter to check messages. I looked around the shop, noticing a back room with a restroom, and a stereo system on another counter with a stack of CDs next to it.

Alana hung up the phone and walked slowly and sexily up to me.

"My aunt out of town till Monday," she said. She put her arms around my neck and tilted her head up to me with slightly parted lips, silently asking for something to make them part even more.

I slowly licked around her lips, and then licked them, tasting strawberry margarita. I kissed her deeply as both hands lowered to her bountiful butt and rubbed gently. I sucked her sweet tongue, and then I sucked her lips, concentrating more on her juicy lower lip. Her body pressed tighter against me as she whimpered. My tongue licked her face, kissing her cute nose. I sucked the tip of it and then kissed her eyelids as she closed them. I sucked her earlobe and went on down to her neck, where I lingered for a moment, gently nipping, all the while still massaging that great ass. I brought one hand up, went under her top, and gently squeezed one of her long nipples.

She held me tighter, saying, "Bay-bee ... Davey ... Bay-bee ... Davey ..."

I looked at that beautiful face as I played with her nipple and butt. Her eyes were closed as she moved her head from side to side, saying my name. Then she opened her pretty, long-lashed eyes.

"Wait minute," she said. She went into the back room and came out with a huge white bearskin rug. She spread it out on the floor. "You like music?" I nodded. She went to the stereo, selected a CD, and put it in. I was surprised—and turned on—by the tune she selected. It was Ravel's *Bolero*. Back in 1979, a movie called *10* was released. It's the movie that made Bo Derek and her cornrows famous. In the movie, Bo's character, Jennifer, tells Dudley Moore's character that she likes to do different things to different music, and to Ravel's *Bolero*, she discloses, she likes to "fuck." She goes on to say it is "the most descriptive sex music ever written."

That music softly filled the air as Alana seductively approached me as I stood in the middle of the rug. I was unbuttoning my shirt when she reached me. She helped me finish. I pulled her T-shirt over her head. Her long hair got tangled in it for a moment. We kissed some more, with her naked breasts pressed against my body. I sucked her tongue and lower lip some more as I tweaked her hard nipples. Slowly she traced her tongue down my body, sucked my lower lip, and nibbled on my neck, and all the while I was running my fingers through her silky hair.

She licked my shoulder and ran her tongue across my chest to my nipples, which she bit gently, and then she went to my navel as she unbuckled my belt, unzipped my fly, and reached a warm soft hand inside my boxers to pull out my rock-hard member. The music in the background—it was on repeat—the rug, the dim lights, and this sensuous woman had me in a dreamlike state. *Is this heaven?* I thought.

She was slowly stroking my dick as she stuck her tongue into my navel and licked my stomach. Then she released my rod for a moment as she pulled my jeans and boxers completely down. Once done, she continued stroking it. My hands were running through her locks. She was on her haunches in front of me now as her tongue went lower. She kissed around my pubic hair, lifted my eight inches, and licked my balls, and then she took one in her mouth and gently sucked.

My hands were going faster and faster through her hair. Her head backed away, and she looked at the penis she was stroking. "You have handsome dick," she uttered, and then she quickly engulfed it. I moaned. She sucked it smoothly for a minute and then backed away and licked the head. "Mmmmm, good," she said. She licked and nibbled up and down each side of it, and then she stuck it back in her mouth, still stroking at the same time.

I looked down at the lovely face and those luscious lips slurping on my dick, and I almost lost it. She was sucking harder, faster, now, as if she couldn't wait to taste my juice, and I got harder and hotter. But I didn't want to come yet. I backed away. She didn't want to let go. Her mouth went with me as I backed up. "No, I want, Bay-bee; I want … Give it back; give it back."

"Later," I said softly. I got down on the rug and laid her on her back. Her black hair was splayed like an outline around her head on the cream-colored rug. I went up to her face and licked her forehead and her eyebrows. I kissed her lids as my hand reached down to the junction between her thighs and rubbed the soft, fine hairs covering her mound. She opened her legs a little more. I kissed her soft DSLs and licked her neck, noticing that she breathed faster whenever I sucked on the left side of her neck.

I lingered there for a moment as one finger slid between her slick lips below and went inside her. She moaned. I licked my way to her nipples and then sucked and nibbled them, letting her feel my teeth as I gently bit down on them. She moaned more. I slipped a second finger inside her tight hole. It was getting more and more lubricated. I withdrew my fingers and brought them to my lips. Her sex smell was fresh. I sucked her juice off my fingers. "Mmmmmm. You taste sweet," I informed her.

"Let me taste," she whimpered.

I returned my fingers to her vagina to gather more of her juice and brought the fingers up to her lips. She sucked them gently and then insistently. "I like. You taste better."

"I'll never know," I said.

"You know," and then she pulled my face down and kissed me hard as my fingers found her wet clitoris and began squeezing it. All I could taste was her in that kiss, and that was all I wanted to taste.

I broke the kiss and traveled down her body, kissing her nipples some more, sticking a tongue in her navel, and licking her hip until I found my way to the top of her neatly trimmed V. I grazed around it and down one smooth thigh, sucked her knee, and went on down her calf to her ankle. I nibbled there for a moment as I brought my wet fingers down and rubbed her juice over her toes.

I then lifted the foot off the rug, scooted down to sit facing her and lowered my head to suck her juice off each toe one by one. When I finished, I put all five toes in my mouth together, sucking on them. She was writhing on the rug. I wasn't done yet. I retrieved some more of her vagina honey on my fingers, smeared it on the toes of her other foot, and then sucked each in turn, culminating with all five toes in my mouth. "Bay-bee!" she shouted.

I worked my way back up the other leg while my hand fondled her hot, wet, slippery clitoris, kissing her knee and the area behind it, then moving up her inner thigh until I came to that sweet junction that housed her power: that sweet, lovely fold of skin that had a soft slit surrounded by lips that couldn't smile but could make a man smile from ear to ear—that sweet, soft slit that, when parted, revealed the entrance to a warm, friendly place that men will do almost anything to visit. The revealed moist pink muscles can constrict, contract, hold you, and let you go, but they will never really let go, even if you're miles away. That was the power that resided at that wonderful female junction.

I looked at her power. It was pretty. She had a pretty pussy with a clitoris that jutted out. It begged to be kissed. I lowered my head, stuck my tongue out, and licked up and down her slit, tasting her warm, slippery, clear emission—her honey. Alana was moaning continuously now, moving her head from side to side. It was music to my ears, coupled with the *Bolero* in the background.

I opened her wet lips with my tongue and pushed my tongue as far into her opening as it could go. I moved my mouth up to her clitoris as my fingers replaced my tongue in her opening. I brushed her clitoris with my tongue gently while pushing back the hood that covered it. Alana rubbed my bald head with one hand while her other hand was patting the rug.

I let the hood again cover her clitoris, and then I sucked on it tenderly, moving my head up and down on it gently, slowly, and then harder, faster, alternating, also intermittently flicking my tongue across the hooded clit. At the same time, I removed one slick, juice-covered finger from her vagina, carefully found her anus, and slowly pushed the finger inside, thankful that I had clipped my fingernails that morning.

Now she rubbed my head with both hands as she wailed. I moaned while I pushed my fingers in and out of both openings and my head went up and down on her rubbery, protruding clitoris. "Mmmmm, you taste so good, Alana. Give it to me; give me your juice," I crooned. "Mmmmmm, give it to me, baby." Over and over I whispered to her as I slurped and licked, until finally I felt her body tense. And then she let out a long, shrill wail as her floodgate opened.

She actually squirted a little as she pulled my head tight up against her; that's how hard she climaxed. I slowed down my motions as her body started relaxing, and she let my head go. She was breathing heavily. We both were sweating. "Oh my, Bay-bee, Davey ... oh my," she said in short breaths. "I never come like that before—never."

"You're twenty-five," I reminded her. "You'll come like that some more."

"With you, yes?"

"With me, yes," I replied. *And with others too,* I knew.

We were lying next to each other with me propped up on my side, looking at her voluptuous body; bronze skin; perfect breasts; brown areolae and taut nipples; small waist; wide hips with the protruding butt behind it; the long, tapered thighs; smooth, shapely calves; and small feet with manicured toes.

She was looking at me, smiling, and then her eyes went down to my half-hard penis. It sprang to attention when she reached for it and started stroking. She crawled on top of me and kissed my lips, still holding on to my member.

"Come take the mustache ride," I bade, lying on my back.

"What's that?"

I reached down, placed my hands on her butt, and pulled her torso up to my face. I lifted her up and placed her vagina on my mouth. "This," I said in a muffled voice as I started licking her slit again while she sat on my face. She leaned back on my propped-up knees, and I partook of her delicious nectar. I just wanted her to sample the ride because I knew that "Junior" had other plans.

"My dick wants you now," I announced.

She must've had the same plans, because she quickly scooted back down my body, having never let go of my hardness, and then she raised up and slowly wiggled herself down on it, enveloping it within her soft, moist, hot walls. "Oooooooh, Davey." She swooned as I thrust up to meet her downward movement. Her pussy made a sucking sound as she rose up to the tip of my penis and plunged back down several times.

"Take it, baby!" I said. "Take the dick!"

She moaned. Without losing contact, I flipped us over so that I could be on top. She brought her knees up toward her breasts, splaying her thighs out, and I began long-stroking her. "Oh, fuck me, fuck me, Bay-bee; fuck me, Davey," she cried. I slowed down, brought the head out to the edge of her vagina, and then quickly pushed it back in. "Ooohhhh, Bay-bee!" she wailed. I did it again. This time I stirred it around her opening briefly, as if I were stirring pancake batter, before pushing it slowly back into her. "Bay-bee, Bay-bee, Bay-bee!" she moaned. "Give me that dick, give me that Black dick!" Hearing the music in the background, I settled into a rhythm, stroking slowly, then thrusting hard and fast, and then slowly again, until she said, "I'm coming, I'm coming! Don't stop!" I began thrusting faster, smacking up against her booty harder and harder, not gently at all, and then she let out her long, shrill wail again.

I lay there on top of her while her breathing slowed down. "You okay?" I asked, looking down at her as some of my sweat dripped on her face.

"Better than okay," she whispered huskily. "You come?"

"No, not yet," I admitted. "I'm saving it for something."

"You Scorpio too?"

"No." I laughed. "I'm Aquarian."

She smiled. "Now I like Aquarian."

She turned over prone, and I ran my hand through her tangled hair and down her wet back to her jutting, luscious, smooth butt. I rubbed and squeezed it. Then my hands went between her legs and fondled her vagina again.

"You bad boy—I mean man," she cooed. I rose up and licked the salty sweat down her spine, coming to the top of the crack of her butt. I continued licking between that crack and lightly across her anus. "Yes, you bad man." I spread the cheeks of her pretty booty and stuck my tongue in her back hole. "You bad, bad man," she said, breathing quickly. I placed my hands underneath her hips and raised her to her knees, with the top part of her body still flat on the rug. Her hands were stretched out in front of her, and her butt was sticking up in the air.

I was behind her on my knees, licking from her anus to her vagina, holding her cheeks apart with my hands. The scent of sex filled the room. In fact, I wouldn't have been surprised if the scent was spreading all over the neighborhood.

Her pussy tastes so good, I thought as I plunged my tongue into it and then stuck it back into her anus. It was tight and tasteless for the most part, and using my tongue on it seemed to turn her on even more. I scooted closer to her, holding my stiff rod. I brushed it up and down her slippery slit and then placed the bulbous head of it at her entrance and pushed it slowly into her vagina. I began pile-driving at a leisurely pace as she got wetter and wetter, and her opening started talking to me as only a wet pussy can. Just the slipping, sloshing, and suction sounds made me harder. "Oh, Bay-bee, Bay-bee, Bay-bee!" she yelled.

"Take the dick, baby; take it. Suck my dick with your pussy!"

She started wiggling and pushing back more frantically, using her muscles to attempt to wring the juice out of my joint. "Put it in my ass!" she pleaded. "Please put it in my ass, Bay-bee."

"You sure?" I asked. I had wanted to do it earlier. I had a feeling she would like it.

"Yes, Bay-bee, Davey," she crooned. "I want it there; I *like* it there."

I backed my dick out of her pussy. "Then ask for it." I said.

"Put it in my ass," she said with little feeling.

"Ask for it, Alana!" I demanded forcefully. I didn't know where it came from, but that was how I suddenly felt when I knew what she wanted. The situation made me think of a chick I once knew named Saturday Knight. "Beg for it!"

"Put it in my ass. Please," she responded with a whimper.

"What do you want in your ass, Alana?"

"Your dick, Bay-bee, Davey; I want your dick in my *ass*."

"*You* put it in," I told her.

She reached between her legs and gripped my penis, which was dripping wet with her goodness, and brought it up to her anus. And then she placed it at the opening and pulled it into her while backing up on it. I felt it pop past the sphincter muscle and into her hotness. She moaned louder, and I began moving in and out again, slowly at first, while she was pushing back on it, seemingly trying to swallow my penis with her beautiful, round, glistening butt.

"Take this Black dick, Alana. Take it in your pretty ass!" I ordered. "Push back and get it all with your pretty ass! Come get it! *Come get it!*"

I remained still as I looked down at the sexy sight of her splayed out on the rug in front of me. She moaned louder with pleasure as she slammed that pretty, plump, juicy apple bottom back and forth against me with her hair flying all over the place. I got more excited watching her breasts jiggling under her and seeing her small waist, her pretty booty with her brown hole engulfing my hard penis as if it never wanted to let it go. I grabbed some of her hair and pulled back on it, reining her in.

Her pussy was even wetter now, as I discovered when I reached between her legs. Her hand was there too, playing with her clitoris and caressing my balls.

"Fuck my ass! Oh, Bay-bee, fuck my ass! Give it to me, Bay-bee, Davey! Come in my ass! Come for me, Bay-bee, Davey!"

"Yeah, Alana, take this dick, baby girl! Take it all; take it all! It's yours! Now give me that ass! Give me that pretty ass!"

"Come in my ass! Give me that cum in my ass!. Please, Davey.

Give me your cum. Give me your cum! Ooooh, that dick feel so good in my ass! Oh, it feels so *good!*"

Her ass was making love to my dick. I suddenly realized this was what she'd wanted all along. All the other sex had been her foreplay to get to this moment—to this stage. She was an anal sex freak. The way she dressed, the way she moved, her walk—it all was designed to draw attention to her booty. Having someone touch her butt was her aphrodisiac. To have someone *in* it was her craving. That realization made me more excited.

And then I was thrusting to the rhythmic beat of Ravel's *Bolero.* As the music built toward its final crescendo, so did I. My strokes got increasingly faster, harder, and deeper as the beat got louder. She must've heard it and felt it too, because she started pushing back harder, faster, taking every inch of my bone inside of her pretty butt, screaming with pleasure, "I'm gonna come!" She moaned in ecstasy, "Yes, yes, yes! I'm gonna cccccccooooooommmmmmmmmmmmeeeeeee!"

Her announcement triggered me. The music reached its big finish, as did I. I exploded. I felt it start at the pit of my stomach, and it came gushing out deep inside her dark hole. And I heard that long, shrill wail again.

Only this time, it came from me.

TABS TELL TAIL TALE

YOU KNOW, WOMEN DON'T SEEM TO KNOW HOW GOOD THEY HAVE IT. Do they? Especially attractive women. Everything is stacked in their favor. They don't have to lift a damn finger. A woman can go into a bar without a dime in her purse and still walk out quenched, sated, or even tipsy if she wants to go overboard with the drinks offered.

Let a man try that. He'd better be meeting his best friend or his boys if he wants some free drinks. In fact, if a man goes into a bar and sees a woman he knows, he'd better be prepared to buy *her* drinks.

Women seem to think that men they know, or men who act like they want to know them, owe them that—as if an interested man's job is to pay for their refreshments if he sees them out somewhere, be it drinks, food, or both.

Can a guy get away with that? Can a guy expect a female friend that he sees out, or a female who seems interested in him, to go into her pocket and pay for his refreshments just because she invited herself to his table or to the seat next to him at the bar?

Hell to the naw!

But a dude had better not invite himself to a female friend's table! He's just asking for trouble if he does. He'd best be ready to begin paying for everything that comes to that table. And the waitress doesn't even ask; she assumes it too.

And women have no problem with this societal arrangement. They seem to think that a man is *not* a *gentleman* if he doesn't go into his pocket to sport her, even if the guy is just a friend and has never hit it, or never even attempted to hit it.

However, if he *is* someone who used to hit it, then she is *definitely* looking for him to go into his pocket, as if her vagina is running a tab, collecting a fee for the times he hit that tail in the past.

Now, Dab, Doc, and I had been frequenting a restaurant called the Stinking Rose in Beverly Hills on LaCienega's Restaurant Row— between Wilshire and San Vicente—on Thursdays for happy hours for several weeks. It's a garlic restaurant. Garlic is a rose that stinks—a stinking rose.

The food there was great. We'd had dinner there several times. But mainly we resigned ourselves to the appetizer menu in the bar area. They had a great garlic chicken with garlic mashed potatoes. And the filet mignon garlic chili was the bomb.

The bartenders and the manager came to know us well because of our regularity, as did the Mexican valets and the valet captain. Whenever they saw us drive up, they would park our rides in prominent spots and not bother giving us claim tickets like the other customers. We were known to tip well too.

We decided to start inviting friends and new ladies that we met to Thursday nights there to have drinks with us. Usually we'd just hang there at and around the bar area, which was separate from the dining area, but they also had a little room—the Red Room—right off the bar area, which had couches and cushions; we'd take our people there too. It used to be a cigar room before they banned smoking in restaurants in Los Angeles.

Eventually hanging there on Thursdays became popular for our crowd. We developed a following, like a clique thing. They all knew that the 3Ds would be at the Stinking Rose on Thursdays after work, so more and more friends, and friends of friends, would come through. It was like our Cheers. Sometimes we would have relationship discussions in the Red Room.

The restaurant had a draw of its own as well. As I said, the food was very good, and occasionally celebrities would pop in to dine or drink. And of course we would very often see some very tasty morsels coming through the bar area to have drinks as they waited for their names to be called for din-din. Of course, we jumped on those.

Now, the main bartender on Thursday was Fifi, a blonde cutie pie. She noticed that Dab, Doc, and I were there regularly and that we had a nice group of friends that showed up on Thursdays *and* that we tipped well. She made it a point to know exactly what each of us liked to drink, and as soon as she saw us walking in, she would make the drinks for us at the bar. And then we noticed that she stopped asking for credit cards to start tabs for us. And on top of that, at the end of the evening when she totaled up our tabs, the total came to about half of what we'd really spent. Her tips got even better then.

"Welcome, my friend," the valet greeted as he opened the door of my black Lincoln LS. I had gotten rid of the diesel Mercedes I used to drive.

"Hey, José," I said as I got out of the car. I excused myself through the folks who were waiting for their vehicles and entered the establishment, smelling the scents emanating from the kitchen. I nodded at the cashier behind the glass counter containing the garlic paraphernalia, shook hands with the manager standing just outside the bar, and strolled into the bar area.

"Hi, Davey," Fifi greeted as she started mixing my drink—a cuba libre with Myers's rum and a splash of Rose's lime juice in a tall glass.

I saw Doc sitting at the bend of the bar with Richard Butts, one of our partners from Rendezvous, the club we ran on Friday nights several blocks up the street. It was about six thirty.

"Hey, fellas," I said as we tapped fists.

"Do you want to see the menu?" asked Fifi as she set my drink in front of me.

"No, Fee, I'll just have the filet mignon chili," I responded. "Thank you."

"What's up, Cuba Libre?" Rich asked. "I hear you got a new girl."

"It wasn't me," Doc denied. "It was probably Dab-ski."

"Where is he anyway?" I inquired.

"He just paged me," said Doc. "He's on the way. You know, he's always at a meeting."

"So tell me about this girl," Rich insisted.

"Ain't nothing to tell," I responded. "She's nice. I like her. Case closed."

"She's *fine*," added Doc, "and the boy is into this girl like I ain't never seen him into a woman. In fact, he tells other ladies that we meet about her. He's whipped-ski."

"I ain't whipped," I objected. "I just like her a lot."

"Have I met this girl?" Rich asked.

"Yeah, you've seen her," Doc apprised, "she came by the club-ski a few weeks ago. Honore."

"Honore? A few weeks ago?" Rich tried to recall her, looking at me. "Oh, the night that you didn't show up at the house for breakfast and you had Evelyn—who I *thought* was your girl—and her friend Annette asking about you?" He laughed. "Yeah, Honore. Yeah, she was representing that night. Good catch, Cuba Libre."

"She'll do in a rush," I said matter-of-factly. I didn't like discussing my relationships with the guys when they involved ladies I felt strongly about. I might talk to Dab and Doc about some of my lesser associations, but when I really cared about a lady, I tended to not like sharing much about our bond unless it was coming unglued.

"Dab said you like being secretive with yo' shit." Rich laughed.

I smiled. "Who told you."

"I just told you Dab said—" began Rich.

"Uh"—Doc put a hand on Rich's shoulder, chuckling—"'Who told you' means 'You got that right' or 'Duh.'"

"Oh yeah, I forgot. Cuba Libre has his own language-*ski*."

We all laughed.

"Very funny-ski," Doc said, chuckling at the reference to him.

"Where did you get that from, anyway?" Rich asked. "Adding *ski* to words?"

"It started when folks were saying 'brewski' for beer," shared Doc, "and then I started calling the fellas Dab-ski, Doug-ski, and Davey-ski. Then it just branched off."

"Yep, his own 'ski' language." I laughed.

"Language-ski," corrected Doc.

"What are you guys talking about?" Dab quizzed, walking up.

"Hey, Dab-ski," Doc greeted. "Where you been?"

"I had to go to a meeting," he replied.

We got a chuckle out of that.

Dab was the meeting-est guy in the world. He always had something going on, he claimed. Someone was always pitching ideas to him about doing something pertaining to making some money. Whether it was the social scene, the apparel business, or a new way of doing things, he was the one being approached. He was very good at putting together business plans though. And if it turned out to be something worthwhile, he'd get us involved.

Fifi brought over a Tanqueray and soda for him.

"I ran into Samantha at the gas station up the street," Dab informed us. "She's on her way over here."

"Not the mooch-ski," Doc said.

"Yep, the mooch," acknowledged Dab, "and one of her cutie-pie girlfriends."

"I ain't never seen that girl pull out her wallet." Rich laughed. "You know some of these chicks leave their purses in the car on purpose so they have an excuse *not* to pay."

"No, she's always flashing her Louis Vuitton," Dab reminded. "She just doesn't *open* it."

"Well, you're the one that use to knock her off," Doc accused. "That's why she figures she can get away with that shit. What's that name she calls you?"

"Mr. Munchie." I laughed. "And it has *nothing* to do with potato chips."

"Yeah, Mr. Munchie," Doc said. "You two belong together. Mr. Munchie and Miss Moochie."

"She don't belong with *me*," Dab protested. "I haven't knocked that off in six months."

"Well, she must think you got it on layaway," I said, "'cause you're still paying on it."

"Yeah, well, that shit is coming to a screeching halt," declared Dab.

"Man, you always say that," Rich reminded. "But when these babes start showing their legs, batting their eyes, and smiling at you, you dig deeper in your pocket. You like being known as 'Big Baller, Shot Caller.' Your ego won't let you stop sporting these chicks. And they count on it."

"Samantha better not count on it tonight," Dab said, motioning for Fifi to come over.

"Why not?" Rich asked.

"You going to order something to eat?" Fifi asked Dab when she reached us.

"Probably later," Dab said. "But, Fee, remember that girl that was here a couple of weeks ago whose stuff I told you to put on my bill?"

"Yeah, yeah," said Fifi, "I know who you mean."

"Well," continued Dab, "she's on her way here. We're not covering her tonight. But don't ask her for a card or anything; just don't let her leave without paying. Okay?"

Fifi chuckled. "Okay, I got you. Another one of your exes?"

"Where you get that from?" Dab inquired.

Fifi walked away laughing.

"Where she get that from?" Dab asked us.

We all laughed.

"You're transparent, man," Rich informed him.

"Yeah, and you've been hitting on Fee-ski, huh?" Doc accused.

"Man, you didn't know?" I asked. "She's White, ain't she? *and* she's a COD."

"I knew it was only a matter of time," admitted Doc.

"Well, the time was a few Thursdays ago," Rich informed us, chuckling. "That was the first time y'all went out together, right? After she got off?"

"Bingo!" I answered for Dab. "And a few times after that. But what's up with Sam and her friend when they get here, Dab?"

"Listen, I ain't sporting her tonight," Dab suggested. "And you guys don't do it either!"

"I ain't!" I agreed.

"Me neither!" Doc complied.

"You don't have to worry 'bout *me*!" Rich chimed in.

"Just let her order whatever the hell they want," Dab conspired, "and when our bill comes, just pay for our stuff and see the look on her face."

"What, uh … what happens if she can't handle her bill?" I asked.

"Then I guess she'll be washing dishes tonight," Dab said. "We gotta teach her a lesson. She can't keep coming around us and expecting us to cover whatever she eats or drinks, even if she has another female with her."

"Yeah," I agreed, "you're right about that."

"She's been doing that for six years or so now," said Doc. "Ever since she was on tour with Doug-ski in the stage play 'The Club'."

"Yep, six years too long," Dab added. "I mean, it's not like we see her out a lot anymore, but whenever we do, *boom*."

"Well, you're the one who started it," I reminded.

"No," Dab corrected, "*you* started it! She called you her big brother."

"Until *you* became 'Big Daddy'!" I laughed along with Doc and Rich.

"Okay, okay," Dab said, giving in, "but tonight I'm not Big Daddy, you're not 'Big Bro,' and you guys—"

"Just innocent stepchildren-ski." Doc laughed.

We continued drinking, chatting, and interacting as acquaintances and other customers started filling up the bar area. Samantha sashayed in with a very pretty brown-skinned honey behind her. They got there just in time to grab the two remaining barstools at the other end of the bar.

After securing their seats, Samantha brought her friend down to our end of the bar. Dab and Fifi exchanged confirmations.

"Hey fellas," Samantha greeted, hugging each of us in turn. "This is my friend Starr."

"Who told you," I said, admiring the exotic-looking beauty. "Nice to meet you, Starr. I'm Davey." I took her hand and kissed it.

"Whew." Starr swooned. "Nice meeting you too, Davey."

"What about me, Big Brother?" Samantha asked, offering her hand.

I brought her hand to my mouth and kissed my own hand. "I don't know where your hand's been, Sam," I joked.

"You don't know where Starr's hand been neither," she reminded.

I grinned. "I don't care where hers been."

Everyone laughed.

After the rest of the introductions were made, Sam and Starr retreated to their stools.

I went to the middle of the bar to get Fifi's attention and told her to find out what Starr was drinking. She came back with the info, and I sent a mojito down to her and went back to the fellas.

I saw Starr look in my direction, hold her mojito up, nod, and smile at me. I nodded and smiled back.

"Uh, wha'chu doing, Cuba Libre?" Rich whispered.

"I'm sending Starr a drink," I whispered back.

"I thought Dab said not to sport them tonight," Rich reminded.

"I ain't listening to Dab." I laughed. "Hell, he probably wants to send Starr a drink himself."

"Yeah," Rich agreed, "she *is* his type."

"Yep, cutie-pie, slender but shapely," I noted, "with nice-size baby-dinners—the way I like 'em too."

"Neither one of you likes ladies with big tits," Rich said. "Just me and Doc like those."

"Exactamundo. Plus I'm only sending her one drink," I shared. "*Plus* Dab is always changing his mind about shit. Big Baller, Shot Caller is in his blood. He'll give in before this night is up."

My prediction proved to be true. Some other CODs we knew showed up and sat at the tables and couches around the bar. Dab bought drinks for a table of three; however, nothing was bought for Sam or Starr.

Sam came over to us a couple of times to chat while she was at our end of the bar, and I went over to Starr to get her contact information. She was more than happy to supply me with her digits even though she was eating.

After I returned to my stool, I saw a couple of guys approach Sam and Starr. I had no problems with that. I had the info I wanted. She would get a call from me in a few days.

"You're gonna wait a few days to call her?" Doc said, sounding surprised, when I mentioned this.

"Yeah, man," I responded. "Look, you never call a COD the day after you meet her, especially these young cutie-pies. You'll seem too anxious. Always wait a few days. Now, with older cutie-pies, you can call them the next day. They *need* to know you're interested as soon as possible. They're ready to give it up. Not the youngsters. Gotta keep them off guard."

"Davey's right about that, y'all," Rich co-signed.

"Hell yeah he's right," Dab added. "That's what makes you a *real* OG."

"Yo' age makes *you* a 'real OG,'" I joked.

There was laughter all around.

Last call was called. We motioned for Fifi to bring our tabs over.

"So we gonna invite some folks over to the pad-ski?" inquired Doc, waiting for Fifi to bring our tabs.

"I don't know. What do you think, Dab?" I asked as I noticed Dab holding up his hand toward us as he watched Sam interacting with Fifi.

We all observed the scene. Fifi handed Sam her tab. Sam looked at it, nodded and smiled, and handed Fifi a credit card. It appeared to be an American Express card. Fifi ran the payment, and Sam signed the receipt. She looked down at us, smiled, and waved as she and Starr departed with the two guys right behind them.

"Here's your tabs, fellas." Fifi handed one to each of us with a smile on her face.

"Let me see the damage," Dab said, looking at his total. "What!"

"Sam got you, huh?" I chuckled.

"Naw," Dab replied. "My tab says zero."

"So does mine," chimed Doc.

"And mine," Rich added.

"Samantha took care of all you guys' food and drinks," said Fifi. Then she looked at me.

"What?" I asked, having not looked at my tab yet. I looked and noted that mine was *not* zero.

"She paid for your stuff too," Fifi explained, "but not the drink and food her girlfriend said you bought for her."

"Females! I only bought her *one* damn drink," I uttered. Everyone burst out laughing, including Fifi, as I pulled out my card, shaking my head.

"Yep," added Dab, "you bought her a drink and asked for her phone number, so she figured she had a right to be on *your* tab. Now it's up to you to go or not go for the tail."

"Naw," I replied. "I can tell it's gonna take me paying quite a few more tabs before she gives up the tail. And the fact that she pulled that move tonight lets me know all I need to know about her. Anybody want a phone number? It's paid for."

There were no takers.

We told the remaining folks in the bar area about our after-party at the Mini-Mansion and headed home with them following us.

And lo and behold, Sam and Starr were waiting in their cars in front of the house when we got there.

Hmmm, I wondered, *who will be getting some tail this night. Me? Dab? Both? Neither?*

THE LADY IS TRIPPIN'

OUR FORMER ROOMMATE, DOUG KENNER, INVITED US TO ATLANTA for his anniversary party. Dab, Doc, and I decided that instead of going to the ATL alone, as we normally did, we each would take a lady along. Usually when we traveled together, it would be just the 3Ds. Sometimes our buddies Richard Butts and Dennis Elliott would go. We called Richard "Dick" to make him a fourth D. "Denn" was our honorary fifth D. And wherever we went, whether it was to the ATL, the Essence Festival, or the Sinbad/Soulbeach Music Festival, we'd wreak havoc on the nightclub scene.

The ATL had a helluva nightclub scene and quite a few nice "booty-shakin' clubs." But since we would be hanging with Doug and Copper on this trip, we thought we might as well have CODs on our arms too.

Now, my predicament was deciding *which* lady I wanted to invite. You see, if I took a trip with a lady, I wanted her to be fine. I wasn't taking no trips with an ug-mo, or a mud duck. No way!

At the time, I was seeing two fine ladies.

Well, actually, I was seeing one—officially.

Unofficially I was seeing two.

The official one was Renee Chapman.

However, Vanessa, my Ebony Fashion Fair model friend, was back in town for a couple of months on a hiatus from touring. So, unofficially, I was creeping with her.

Renee had some issues. Ever since that night she came by the house and Vanessa was there, she sensed that I was seeing someone else besides her. I don't know where she got that smell from. I couldn't understand how a notion like that got into her head. What could've possibly made her think that? I had always been very discreet when I took Vanessa out after she got back in town. We went all the way down to Orange County, where I was more unlikely to run into someone I knew.

Even with her issues in mind, I decided that since I'd been seeing Renee longer and she was familiar with the ladies that Doc and Dab were taking, I would ask her to come along.

Initially she agreed. However, a couple of days later, when I was at her place, her availability changed.

"Baby," she asked me as we were lying in bed, "what day are you guys going to Atlanta?"

"Two weeks from now," I informed her. "Why?"

"I don't think I'll be able to go."

"Oh yeah?" The image of Vanessa suddenly popped into my head. "Why not?"

"I got a call this morning from my mother. She and Daddy are coming to town that weekend, and they're going to stay with me. I can't run out of town on them."

"Oh no," I said with an inner smile, "that wouldn't be right."

"But I don't want to disappoint you either."

"Hey, li'l girl, I understand. These are your parents. It's all right. I'll just go by myself. It's no biggie."

"But aren't Dab and Doc taking Siramad and Angie?"

"Maybe. Keep in mind Angie is married. She may not be able to get away. And Doc don't have a second choice."

"Do *you* have a second choice?"

"My second choice is my first choice," I said pointedly.

"That's sweet." She pushed her butt back at me as we spooned on top of the covers with my arms around her waist.

And my actual first choice is Vanessa.

It had been over a year since the Speakeasy incident with Vanessa, and I still hadn't closed the deal. This was mainly because she wasn't in town a lot, and when she *was* here in LA, she was busy. Friends and family were always pulling her in so many directions.

We'd managed to get together once for lunch and another time for drinks. We'd talked about finding time to get together again so we could consummate our relationship, but that time hadn't come yet.

I called her the next day from my office.

"Hey you," she greeted when she recognized my voice.

"'Hey you' back at ya," I replied.

"Have you found time for me yet?" she asked.

"You're the one." I chuckled. "Miss Popular-Always-in-Demand."

"Yeah, that's true." She sighed. "I think I need to get away from these folks for a few days." She laughed.

"Funny you should say that," I began. "Doug is having an anniversary party in Atlanta, and he invited me and the fellas down there. We're going to be staying at his place."

"Doug? Your ex-roommate? Star of the hit sitcom *Shelter Skelter*?"

"That be him." I laughed.

"I wanna go!" she wailed.

"Well, you gonna go."

"I am?"

"If you want to."

"Driving or flying?"

"Flying."

"Yes, I wanna go. How do I get my ticket?"

"I'll get your ticket."

"That's so sweet of you. When are we leaving?"

"Two weeks from now. We're flying out Thursday after next, coming back early the following Monday."

"Great! It'll be good to see Doug again and good to get away from here."

"And good to be with me?"

"It'll be *better* than good."

"Watch out, girl!"

"*You* watch out!" she said sensuously. "Hey, now I gotta go shopping to get some new stuff! I'll talk to you later?"

"You got it."

I hung up smiling from ear to ear and called the airline to book the same flight that Dab and Doc had booked earlier. I was told that I should get the tickets in the mail in a few days. Everything was set in motion. It was just a little more motion than I had anticipated.

"Your ticket arrived today," Doc informed me the next Thursday as I walked in the door after work. Keep in mind, this was the mid-90s.

"You mean tickets," I corrected, opening the envelope that was in the mail slot.

"Tickets? I thought you said Renee's not going-ski," he insinuated.

"She's not," acknowledged I.

"So who are you taking?"

"Yeah, who are you taking?" Angie asked, coming out of the downstairs bathroom.

"You'll see," I told them, as I put my briefcase on the hall table and placed the envelope inside.

The fellas didn't know about me seeing Vanessa; it was still on the hush-hush. I didn't want the word to get out until we got out … of town. And I *definitely* didn't want Renee to get wind of anything. She got along very well with Angie and Siramad—especially Angie. I didn't want Angie opening her big mouth.

"Angie wouldn't do that-ski," Doc assured me after Angie had left.

"I wouldn't think so," I agreed, "since she's a married woman sneaking around. *But* she *is* a woman, and she likes Renee, and women tend to look out for each other."

"Yeah, that's true," he admitted, "but I'll have a talk with her. So who you taking?"

"Vanessa."

"Vanessa! You lucky dawg-ski! Dab's gon' be jealous as hell. How long has this been goin' on?"

"Well, ain't nothing really going on," I corrected. "I saw her a couple of times since that night you guys *and* Renee walked in on us last year when Fashion Fair was in town. If you guys had gone to Li'l J's like you said you were, something woulda gon' down *that* night."

"Well, hopefully something *or someone* will go down-ski in Atlanta-ski."

"Who told you," I said. We both laughed.

The week before the trip, Renee told me that she really felt bad about not being able to go to Atlanta with us and that she was considering letting her parents stay at her place and fend for themselves while they were in Los Angeles.

I assured her that I was okay with going solo to the ATL and that she should stay in town and make sure her parents had a fun visit.

"You sure you gonna have a good time down there?" She asked as we were having drinks at the Stinking Rose on the Thursday before the trip. We were seated at our usual spot at the bar next to Doc, Dab, and his main lady, Siramad.

"I ain't sure, baby," I said, thinking about Vanessa, "but I'm gon' try."

"Davey-ski will be all right." Doc laughed on the other side of Renee. "We're used to him being the fifth wheel. Before he hooked up with you, he was known for that."

There were other folks we knew sitting at tables near the bar and at the other end of the long bar. We had just started our regular Thursday happy hour routine at the garlic restaurant. More of our friends had heard about it and were beginning to patronize the spot on Thursdays. The manager and bartenders were aware that the increase in patrons on Thursday was due to us. Consequently, Fifi and the other bartenders gave Dab, Doc, and me special treatment with prices, even giving us free drinks at times.

I didn't know, however, that Vanessa knew about the spot. I found that out when I looked up and saw her walking in with her sister, Venita, and another sexy lady. They took a seat at a table in the corner.

"Those are some beautiful ladies," Renee said.

Just then, the two sisters saw me and the fellas. They waved and blew us a kiss. Dab, Doc, and I waved back. Doc went over to their table.

"Isn't that that Fashion Fair girl?" Renee asked.

"Uh, yeah," I responded, "I guess she's back in town."

A loud laugh came from their table, and I heard the word *Atlanta*. Renee smiled. "Mm hmm. You didn't know?"

"Why would I know?" I asked. "The fellas didn't mention it."

"Those are some *fun* girls," Doc commented when he came back to his bar seat.

"Yeah, they all right," I said matter-of-factly.

Renee just looked at me.

As agreed, she followed me back to the house after we all left the Stinking Rose. We had made plans for her to spend the night. I saw my briefcase still on the hall table when we walked in. I retrieved it and took it on up to my bedroom, walking behind Renee. That girl had one sexy walk.

We were both tired and a little tipsy from the drinks, and we got undressed and fell asleep almost immediately without any sexy stuff. I awoke in the middle of the night to start some sexy stuff, but she was in the bathroom. I attempted to wait for her to return to the bed, but my tired, drunk ass fell back to sleep before she arrived.

In the morning, I tried to get something going with her, but we both had to shower, dress, and get to our respective offices. In fact, Renee was rushing more than I thought she had to. I just shrugged it off as preparation for a busy day at work ahead.

The next several days before the trip were a tangled mess for me. Vanessa called me the next day to tease me about not coming over to her table at the Stinking Rose. We talked on the phone just about every day, as she was asking more about our arrangements in Atlanta. We got together for lunch in Long Beach that Saturday.

And Renee was all over me too, calling every day. We got together Saturday night and then Sunday for a movie. She wanted to see as much of me as she could before her folks got in Tuesday, two days before I was leaving for Atlanta.

I was being pulled in two different directions, and I had no one to blame but myself. The fact that I was getting away for a few days with Vanessa made it a little palatable. Thursday morning finally came.

Dab and Doc had Siramad and Angie come by the house and leave their cars in the driveway. I didn't want to take that chance with Vanessa's car. I didn't want Renee driving by and seeing a car she didn't recognize parked at the house. So we were going to pick her up in Holliday's Range Rover on the way to the airport. Luckily, her house was not far off the airport route.

"So who are we picking up, man?" Dab asked as we headed out.

I smiled. "You'll see."

"Why the big mystery?" Dab continued.

"It won't be a mystery long." Doc laughed. "She'll be getting in the car-ski in a few minutes."

"Oh," Dab said, "so you know who it is?"

"Yep," Doc said smugly.

"Well, it's definitely not Renee," Angie deduced, "'cause she lives in the other direction, in Baldwin Hills."

"Nope," I volunteered, "it's not Renee."

"Hmpff!" Angie snorted.

"Well, whoever she is," Siramad said, "I hope she's gonna be fun."

"She'd better be," I joked.

"Oh, you don't know?" Dab asked.

"Oh, I know," I corrected, "I definitely know."

"Here we are," announced Doc as he pulled into Vanessa's driveway. She lived in a house off Airport Boulevard and Manchester in a quiet little neighborhood several blocks from the airport.

I got out of the car to ring her doorbell, but she came out with her luggage before I could take two steps.

"Vanessa!" I heard Dab exclaim.

"Yep, Vanessa-ski," Doc confirmed.

"Hey, lady," I greeted.

"Hey, man," she replied as she kissed me on the cheek.

I put her luggage in the back, opened the back door for her, and slid in beside her. There was a minimum of conversation after I introduced her to the other two ladies. They were both very friendly to Vanessa. Actually, I had expected that from Siramad; she was cool like that.

We parked the car in Lot 6 and took the shuttle to the airport, checked the bags in at the curb, and proceeded to our gate. It was about ten o'clock on a Thursday morning, so it wasn't very crowded there. Quite a few folks were milling around at the gate when we checked in.

For some reason, I was feeling a strange vibration that whole morning. It got stronger as we got closer to the airport, and even stronger as we entered the terminal and headed to our gate. It was some type of foreboding.

And then I found out what it was.

"You're *not* getting on that plane with her!" A female voice rang out as the six of us headed to the line to board the plane.

"Somebody's in trouble." I said to the group, chuckling as I looked around to see which one of the passengers was having a dispute.

That's when I noticed that Doc, Dab, Angel, and Siramad were looking at me with strange expressions on their faces.

"You ain't going nowhere!" the female voice announced.

I saw Doc and Dab pointing behind me.

I turned and saw Renee approaching us—rapidly.

"What do you think you're doing?" she asked when she reached me and Vanessa, positioning herself between us.

"Uh, getting ready to board the plane," I answered coolly.

"And who is this!" Renee indicated Vanessa on her left as I stood on her right.

"She's getting on the plane too," I replied, still calm.

"With who?"

"With us." I indicated the rest of the group, who were now off to the side close by.

"With *who?*"

"With us."

"With *who!*" she shrieked. Now she had the attention of everyone in the terminal.

"With *me!*" I said intently, looking her square in the eye.

Renee slapped the hell out of me. I actually saw stars, as if I were a cartoon character.

"Davey," Vanessa said.

"Go ahead and board the plane," I said to her. "Dab, Doc, y'all go on and get her on the plane."

"Hey, buddy—" Dab began.

"Get on the damn plane!" I broke in. "And take Vanessa. I got this."

"You *got* this?" Renee repeated as the fellas backed away with the ladies toward the boarding line. "If that bitch get on that plane, you ain't got *this!* Not anymore! Don't get on that plane, bitch!"

Vanessa stopped and turned toward her.

"Look," she said calmly, "I don't know what's going on. I'm just going on a trip."

"You're going with my man, bitch!" Renee snarled.

"Well, that's between you and him," Vanessa countered.

"You're between me and him!"

"No, I'm not," informed Vanessa. "We're just friends."

"You fuck your friends, bitch?" Renee asked.

"No, I don't!" Vanessa answered. "And you should talk to Davey, not me. My daddy used to tell me that only a fool argues with a fool."

Renee made a move toward Vanessa. I reached out my arm to block her, and she tried to slap me again. I grabbed her wrist before her hand reached my face.

"No more hitting," I said calmly. I was trying to be cool because I didn't want anyone calling the police or security. Hell, I wanted to go to Atlanta—with Vanessa—even though I knew now that my Renee relationship might be on the way out. Or was it? "Renee, we can talk when I get back, but I'm getting on that plane, and you're gonna calm down and stop causing a scene here at the airport."

Over her shoulder, I saw Vanessa and the rest of the group showing their boarding passes and getting on the plane while casting looks back at me.

"Get your hands off me!" she screamed. "I'll be here when y'all get back, Vanessa! Right *here!* Yeah, I *know* your name! I remember you!" She was yelling at Vanessa's back as Vanessa moved to board.

A Delta gate employee called out from her post at the check-in station. "Is everything all right over there?"

"Yes," I responded over my shoulder. "Tell her everything is all right, Renee."

"Yes!" she said reluctantly.

"You're *at* the *airport*, Renee," I reminded her

"Yes, everything is okay now," she announced again to the Delta employee.

"Renee, what's wrong with you? I can't believe this is happening."

"You made it happen, Davey." Tears were beginning to flow.

"Or maybe *you* did," I offered. "Think about it." I had to confuse her—get her to reflect. The thinking process usually calms a person down when he or she is thrown off. A frown appeared on her face. "I'll call you when I get to Atlanta. I gotta go."

I turned to head to the boarding area. She just stood there and watched, not saying a word.

Vanessa was highly upset. When I sat next to her, she rolled her eyes and grunted. "This is the second time I've had another-woman drama when I've been with you," she reminded me. "I don't know if I'm liking this."

"Vanessa," I began softly and distinctly, "I'm not liking it either. I didn't want anything or any*body* disrupting this trip with you. All I want to do is have fun in Atlanta with *you* and everyone. So, please, forgive me for what just happened. I promise that I will not let anything like this happen again. There will be *no mo' drama.*"

"You don't know that" was her nonsmiling response.

I left it alone during the flight. The rest of them had drinks and chatted as I replayed the ordeal in my mind and drifted off to sleep. I like doing that on long flights; it makes the flight go by quicker.

We arrived in Atlanta, picked up the rental SUV, and headed to Doug's place in Alpharetta without a word about the fiasco at LAX. It seemed everyone wanted to leave it alone until we were more relaxed.

Doug greeted us as soon as we reached the front door of his big house in Champions Overlook.

"Y'all made it," he greeted as we streamed into the foyer area of his sixty-five-hundred-square-foot house.

"Nice pad-ski," Doc commended. "You left the Mini-Mansion for a maxi-mansion." Everyone laughed.

Doug hugged and greeted each of us. He knew all the ladies from his days as our roommate in LA.

"Long time, no see," he directed at Vanessa. "How's Venita doing?" Venita had always had a special liking for Doug.

"She's doing great," Vanessa answered. "She wanted to come too."

"She could've," said Doug. "That's my li'l sistah. The guys in Atlanta would've treated her like a queen."

Doug showed us around the spacious house, including his well-furnished large basement with pool table, and theater room with plush leather seats; and then he took us up to our bedrooms. The ladies decided to unpack as the guys and I headed back downstairs to have a drink at the backyard bar around the swimming pool and Jacuzzi.

"So where's Copper?" I asked, as Doug made drinks for Dab and Doc and a cuba libre with Myers's rum for himself and me.

"Oh, she's still at work," replied Doug. "She plans to fix a big dinner for you guys and some other folks she's inviting Sunday afternoon."

"Cool," I replied, "'cause I'm treating everyone to dinner tonight. What's a good restaurant for steaks in Atlanta?" My Stein and Frank Agency was having a great year, plus I wanted to impress Vanessa.

"There are quite a few good ones," Doug replied, "but I really like the service at Fleming's by Perimeter Mall. I'll make reservations. So what's this chatter I'm hearing about LAX?"

We filled him in on the airport incident as we sat at the bamboo bar he had built around his barbecue grill. There were bamboo tables, cushioned chairs, and couches spread around the large backyard, which housed a hot tub, rock formations, a few palm trees, and a small waterfall flowing into a saltwater pool.

"What I wanna know is how she knew which airline, what time, and what gate?" Dab pondered.

"Probably that nosey Angie," I speculated, looking at Doc.

"I don't think so, Davey-ski," Doc shook his head, "because purposely, I never told her, just so something like that couldn't happen."

"Where did you keep your tickets, Davey?" Doug asked.

"In my briefcase," I answered, "and there's no way she had a chance to get near it. It *had* to be Angie!"

"Well, I'll tell you one thing," Dab informed us, "those girls have definitely bonded behind yo' mess."

"What you mean?" I asked.

"They've bonded," Dab repeated. "Siramad and Angie were all pro-Renee before, but I heard them talkin' to Vanessa on the plane and telling her how they liked the way she handled the situation and apologizing for Renee's behavior and saying how they couldn't believe that she'd do that."

"Yeah," Doc agreed, "they're *both* all for Vanessa now-ski. That's why I can't believe Angie had anything to do with it."

I didn't know what to believe, but I knew that I wanted to get back in the good graces—*and* get to the good embraces—of Vanessa. I did not want to be in Atlanta with her not feeling affectionate. I had to get back on her good side.

Copper came in looking great. She was a beauty beyond compare, having long, dark sandy hair with a widow's peak; light brown exotic eyes with gold flecks; full lips; a great smile with dimples; and a body that made a man look and keep looking. Just her presence in her home, being the accommodating hostess after introductions, made everyone feel at ease and comfortable and glad to be there with her outgoing personality. She made me think of Renee, whom I'd always maintained had a slight resemblance to Copper. *Someday maybe they'll meet*, I thought.

We got in the SUV and headed to Fleming's for dinner.

There were quite a few people there waiting for their names to be called when we arrived. I asked Vanessa to stroll through the outside mall area with me as the others waited.

"So are you ever going to forgive me?" I inquired as we enjoyed the warmth of the setting sun and the evening breeze.

Vanessa smiled. "I want to. But will you let me forgive you? All the girls are telling me what a nice guy you are. I already know that! We've been friends for years. I was digging you when you didn't even know it. But whenever I let myself try to be with you, something happens."

"I know, I know. Funny, ain't it?"

"Nope, it's *not* funny. Is something, someone, trying to tell us something?"

"Naw, naw, naw. It's just bad timing on my part. I'm with someone else but can't get you off my mind."

"And what do you have in mind for me?"

"What do you want me to have in mind?"

"I mean, is it just sex you want? 'Cause I gotta tell you, I'm in and out of town a lot—mostly out. And there *is* a guy that I'm seeing out of town. But there's something about you too. However, I'm not looking for a one-on-one relationship, and I do *not* want to mess up yours."

"Wow. Girl, you're turning me on even *more!*"

We both laughed.

"I don't like drama, though," she added.

"Neither do I," agreed I. "Neither do I."

"But I *do* like teddy bears," she appended as we stood in front of a gift shop's window display.

"Well, let me hook a sistah up!" I suggested. We both laughed again.

There was a Bank of America ATM next to the shop. I decided to kill two birds with one stone. I figured I'd get some cash out to make the gift purchase *and* have cash to tip the Fleming's valet after dinner.

I inserted my credit card and entered my PIN and the amount I wanted. A message appeared on the screen saying that the machine was confiscating my card.

"What the hell!" I exclaimed.

"What's wrong?" asked Vanessa.

"This damn ATM took my Visa!"

Just then I heard a shrill whistle. Doc was a half a block away, waving for us to come back.

I decided to handle the ATM situation later, since it was after banking hours and I still had my MasterCard and American Express.

We headed back to the restaurant, where we had an amazing dinner. My filet mignon was the best I've ever had. Doug suggested we all share four chocolate lava cake desserts. Aw, man, I wanted to order another one to go. I was addicted.

Our server brought our tab, and I indicated for him to hand the black leather folder to me. The total was well over $600 with the 20 percent tip that I always included. He took my MasterCard and disappeared as we continued with our friendly banter at the table. Everyone was in a great mood.

The server returned without the folder or my card and bent down to whisper in my ear.

"Uh, sir, your card was declined."

"Say what?" I asked out of the side of my mouth, without moving my lips.

"Your credit card was declined, sir," he repeated politely.

Some of my folks were looking at me questioningly. They couldn't hear what was said, but they were smart people. Doug and Dab were reaching for their wallets. I shook my head slightly and stood up.

"I'll be right back." I went to the cashier's desk with the waiter, retrieved my card, handed them my American Express and returned to the table.

"Anything wrong-ski?" Doc asked.

"Naw." I chuckled. "They made a mistake."

"Looks like they're still making them," Angie sneered as the waiter returned to the table and whispered in my ear again.

"American Express wants to speak with you," he informed me.

I followed him to the cashier's podium. The cashier handed me the phone.

"Hello?" I began.

The friendly American Express rep, Barry, introduced himself and asked me to do the same. He then inquired about places and activities where I had recently used the card, and of course, I gave the correct answers.

"My apologies, Mr. Stein," the rep went on. "I'm satisfied that you are indeed the cardholder. The alert is lifted. You can continue utilizing your card."

"So what caused all this?" I asked.

"Well, you or someone called to report the card lost or stolen this morning."

"Oh really? I think I know who that 'someone' is," I reflected, thinking of the Renee incident at the airport. "Well, thank you, Barry, American Express is definitely my favorite card now, and I will *never* leave home without it."

I gave the phone back to the cashier. She completed the transaction, and I returned to the table with my card.

Everyone was looking at me questioningly.

"It's okay, y'all," I informed them as I slid next to Vanessa. "Apparently *someone* reported my credit cards stolen this morning."

"Who would do *that*?" Copper asked, unaware of the Renee incident.

"A very *angry* woman," Vanessa volunteered. There were a few chuckles around the table.

Doug brought Copper up to date regarding the earlier airport incident.

"Wow, Davey, you be careful, my friend," she beseeched. "You guys are Doug's brothers. We can't have anything happening to any of you."

Amens were uttered by all.

We left there and headed downtown to Mr. Vee's on Peachtree, where we danced and drank until the wee hours, ending up at R. Thomas, farther up Peachtree, for early-morning omelets.

That night Vanessa and I just hugged and snuggled through the night in the bed that we shared. I was finally in bed with her, but

I still felt some tension, so I didn't attempt to push. Plus we were tired and tipsy anyway. I figured I'd take it slow. We still had Friday, Saturday, and Sunday nights to go.

Copper and the ladies prepared a helluva brunch the following morning. It was a warm June day, so we were soaking up the sun in the spacious backyard as we ate and drank. We all were in a great mood, laughing and enjoying the atmosphere.

The phone rang.

"Davey!" Copper called out from the kitchen. "It's for you."

"For me? Who is it?"

"Who's calling?" I heard her ask. There came a hesitant "Ohhhh." And then, to me, she said, "It's, uh, Renee."

The mood changed. It got quiet. Everyone looked at me.

"Uh, tell her I'm busy, please."

"He can't come to the phone now," Copper informed the caller. "Okay, I'll tell him. Goodbye."

Copper came back outside with a pitcher of orange juice.

"How did she get this number-ski?" asked Doc.

"Probably the same way she got my flight info and my credit card info—my briefcase," I informed, having thought about it overnight. "What did she say?"

"She said she'll be there waiting," shared Copper.

"Oh boy." I sighed.

We went to the High Museum to hear some jazz that evening and then had dinner at Sambuca before going over to Dominique's new location on Peachtree for some partying.

Vanessa would not let me snuggle with her that night in bed.

The next morning, the fellas and I fixed breakfast for the ladies. A good mood abounded again.

The call from Renee came a couple of hours later, as we were playing bid whist. Doug and Copper weren't the types to tell her to stop calling. Plus Renee was polite each time. However, I didn't talk to her. She left the same message.

That afternoon, the ladies went shopping at Phipps Plaza and

Lenox Mall. Dab and Doc talked Doug and me into going to Magic City.

Personally, I never liked the idea of going to strip clubs to let ladies try to excite me, but Dab insisted on buying me a couple of lap dances from two different dancers to get my mind off my woman problem. I took the dances in stride. They never fazed me. My mind stayed on my woman problem.

We all went to the Lobster Bar for dinner and afterward moved to the Shark Bar on Peachtree, which used to be the Parrot, to dance and drink.

That night Vanessa slept on the couch in our bedroom.

Okay, I thought as I lay there in the bed, looking across the room at her sexy ass over on the couch, *I can't let Renee mess up my weekend. Tomorrow I'm going to be smooth and easy and assure Vanessa that Renee will* not *be at the gate in LA waiting on us Monday afternoon. And if she is, I will handle it and put her in her place. I'm sleeping in the same bed with Vanessa tomorrow night, and we are gon' be all over each other!*

Monday came. We headed back to LA. I'd always liked going to Atlanta, but regardless of that, getting back to Los Angeles was a great feeling.

Upon arrival, we all deplaned from the Delta jet and headed toward the baggage claim, still chatting about the great time we'd had in the ATL, especially the dinner party that Copper put together for us that Sunday evening. That girl can cook. We had played cards and some board games, told jokes, and ate and drank an abundance of alcohol. *Big* fun.

I made a point of looking around for Renee as we got to the gate. She was nowhere to be found, of course. I really hadn't expected to see her. My feeling all along was that she was just talking shit, attempting to make me feel uncomfortable enough not to enjoy myself in Georgia.

Her psychological phone calls hadn't dampened my mood. We had nothing to be anxious about upon getting back to LA. We could enjoy our Sunday and be together Sunday night after the party and wake up contented Monday morning. That's what I had wanted to share with Vanessa that Sunday.

Too bad I hadn't been able to do that. Too bad she'd talked Copper into driving her to the airport while I was still asleep. Yep, she caught a flight back to LA early that Sunday afternoon. She missed out on some good cooking.

THE NAME IS FAMILIAR, BUT ...

BOREDOM.

It didn't happen often to me, but it happened. Usually it occurred when I was in between relationships or when the excitement had gone out of my current relationships. And at the same time, Doc and Dab were deeply involved with their new stuff and always had said stuff over at the house or were otherwise spending a lot of time with those conquests. So I'd go to movies alone, or if there were no movies I wanted to see, I'd catch up on my reading.

Or if I was really, really bored, I'd go through my little black books. I would pick out a lady or two who I hadn't talk to for a while and give them a call. I would usually choose ladies that I'd been intimate with and still got excited about. Or, if I felt frisky, I'd choose someone I had wanted to get intimate with but had never closed the sale.

You see, I maintain that getting with a female is like making a sales presentation. You meet the prospect. You ask open-ended questions to see where she's coming from and to find her hot buttons—or cold ones. And then you make your presentation, overcome her objections, and close the deal.

Simple.

Well, it's not really that simple, because, as I mentioned, there were many ladies in the several little black books that I'd compiled through the years who had objections I *couldn't* overcome. They were the ones who got away—the deals I couldn't close. But, as I'd gotten to be a better salesman through the years, I realized that I probably wasn't using the right sales pitch.

So getting really bored sometimes allowed me the opportunity to go back and rekindle or repitch some prime prospects that got away *and* the ones that got away before I wanted them to. The only problem was that some of them had gotten wiser also.

Hmm, Wanda Gurley. She has three stars by her name.

"Hello?"

"Hey, Wanda! How's everything going?"

"Who's this?"

"Who do you think it is, li'l girl?"

"Ah, there's only one person who says 'li'l girl'"

"Yeah?"

"Davey? Davey Stein!"

"You got it, li'l girl."

"How've you been?"

"Fine, but I've gotten over it."

She chuckled. "Yeah, it's Davey all right."

"How about you?"

"Oh, I'm *still* fine. I haven't changed that much in a year."

"Hmmm, that means you're still the sexiest, shapeliest girl I've ever laid mouth on."

"You got that right, honey." She laughed.

"The way you say 'honey' always sends a tingle through my body."

"The way you say 'body' sends a tingle through my honey," countered Wanda.

"All right now, don't start no stuff. You still live in the same place?"

"Uh, yeahhhhhhh."

"Well, I'll be right on over—"

"Uh, Davey—"

"I'll stop at the store—"

"Davey."

"And get a bottle of—"

"Daveeeeeeeeeeeey."

"Yeah?"

"It's been over a year since I've seen you. I'm not that girl I used to be."

"What do you mean?"

"I mean we never went out. You'd just bring over a bottle of Kendall-Jackson and we would watch a movie for a while and then we'd be all over each other."

"Didn't you like?"

"Yes, I liked, but I also like for a person to take me out to dinner, to a movie, to concerts, to plays … spend money on me, show me they like me for other things besides a bed partner."

"I see."

"So I made up my mind that I will not sleep with anyone until we've gone out for at least a month."

"A month?"

"*A month!*"

"But you and I have already slept together, Wanda."

"That was the old Wanda. This is the new Wanda."

"Don't make me beg you," I joked, "'cause I *will*."

She laughed. "That used to work, but like I said, this is the new Wanda."

"Well, *New Wanda*, the old Davey will call you back—in a month." *Click.*

So much for her. Now, she was good. We had sexual fun together. And we *did* go out at the outset. She must've forgotten that first two weeks. It had just settled into me coming by and us getting busy. I wanted to pick up where we left off, not start all over again. Actually, I stopped seeing her because she was getting too possessive anyway. *Forget Wanda!*

Let's see … Oh yeah, Betty Hymes, three and a half stars.

"Hello?"

"Hello. Is Betty in?"

"Mommy! Some *man* wants you!"

"Hello?" a feminine voice greeted.

I was still thinking about Wanda's stuff, so I almost made that unforgiveable mistake of calling a woman by the wrong name. "Hey, Wan … uh … *Betty!* Betty, Betty, Betty. How's it going, Betty?" I said, trying to cover my slip of the tongue.

"Who is this?"

"Now see? You used to tell me you could always recognize my voice."

"Well, it sounds like Davey Stein, but I know it can't be him, because he usually calls me around one o'clock at night after he couldn't catch anything out at the clubs."

"Well, uh, hmm … well, uh … that was the, uh … the old Davey."

"Oh yeah? Well, uh, this is the new *Wan* … uh … *Betty!*" *Click.*

Hmmmmm. Maybe it's time to call someone I haven't been intimate with.

Now, don't get me wrong. I'm not a playa. I never told either of those two ladies that they were my one and only. They understood. I mean, both were attractive in their own ways, but neither had that special something—that extra ingredient I needed to make me think that she was the one. And if she's not *the* one, then she's just *another* one.

I put aside my current black book for the last year and a half and pulled out my book for the previous two years. And what a two-year period! It was at the beginning of that stint when the 3Ds and I started doing the promotion at Rendezvous on Friday nights. And around the same time, I moved into the Mini-Mansion with Dab, Doc, and Doug.

This edition of my little black book had some interesting memories. I saw Wanda Gurley's and Betty Hymes's names in this book too. After each two-year period, when I started a new book, I would transfer the names and numbers of only those ladies that I was still talking to or interested in, leaving all the people I no longer communicated with out of the updated book. "Last year's stock," I called them.

As I scanned each page in alphabetical order, some of the names elicited a positive or negative reaction in my memory chamber. The positives caused smiles. Some of the negative brought forth laughs. The negatives didn't make the cut for the next year's edition.

I made notes on the ones I was going to consider calling. And then, toward the end, I saw the name "Maura Westover (Libra)." She had four stars.

Now, Libra is my favorite sign. Every Libra lady I've ever known has been a special person—stimulating in every way. We had a lot in common, and the sex was out of this world. Although I've read that Sagittarians are supposed to be the best bedmates for us Aquarians, I've always given my nod to Libras. But for the life of me, I couldn't remember who Maura Westover was.

What does she look like? Is she a COD? She must be; she has four stars! Did we go out? Where did I meet her? Did I meat her? Nothing. I can't remember nuttin'.

I knocked on every door in my memory chamber, but there was no movement whatsoever. Nothing even looked out through the peephole.

So I had only one recourse. I had to call her.

Now, you can't phone a female and tell her that you don't remember who she is. Her fragile ego can't handle that, especially if you went out with her—even more especially if you had sex with her. I had to get *her* to refresh my memory without her knowing she was doing it. I took a deep breath and dialed her number.

"Hello?" a soft voice answered.

"Hello, is, uh, Maura in?"

"She's speaking."

"Hey there, how are you doing? I thought that was you."

"Who's this?" I detected a smile in her voice.

"This is Davey—Davey Stein." I waited for a reaction. There was silence for a long second.

"Well, well," she finally responded, "this *is* a surprise. Long time no see."

"See!" She said "see." So that means we at least laid eyes on each other before. Now what else was laid on each other?

"Well, it really hasn't been *that* long," I probed.

"Hmm, maybe my concept of time is different from yours. Two and a half years constitutes a long time to me."

Ah-ha, an educated lady, I mused.

"I'm surprised you still have my number," she continued.

"I always keep the numbers of good people," I claimed, remembering that her name and number weren't in my current black book. *Why was that? She has four stars! Why didn't she make the cut? Was it another oversight?* I had done that before—not transferred a name that I meant to, simply because the name was near the end of the previous book and I had gotten distracted.

"Okay, so what made you decide to call my number today?"

"Well, uh, I'm doing this nightclub on Fridays in Beverly Hills. It's called Rendezvous, and I'm, uh, calling old friends to, uh, invite them and a guest to come to the club as *my* guests."

"If you remember correctly, I'm not that much of a club person. I prefer art exhibits, jazz concerts, museums, spoken word, plays—stuff like that."

That doesn't ring a bell, I ruminated. *More info is needed.*

"Well, we do offer jazz in the early part of the evening. C'mon, I'm sure you have a girlfriend or two who'd want to get out to a nice club."

"You know, I have heard of Rendezvous. What do you mean you're doing it?"

"Me and some friends are running it on Fridays. I'll put you on my VIP list for this coming Friday; that means you and your guest will be admitted free and you'll have access to the VIP room. What do you say?"

"Hmm. Hold on for a minute and let me call my friend."

"A female friend, right?"

"Of course a female. I *know* you don't want *me* to come to your club with a guy."

"I prefer you come with a female."

"Well, I prefer to come with a female too." She chuckled. "Hold on."

There was silence while she apparently depressed the switch

hook to make another call. I figured that instead of trying to get with her today, as I had done with the previous two women I'd called, whom I'd already been with, I would just invite her to the club first and make my move on her then. That way I could see who she was, impress her with the VIP treatment, and have her doing "favors" for me to have the treatment continue. As Dab would say, "Impress a cutie with bling and you can get the ping without really giving up a thing."

Maura came back on the line. "Okay, I talked to my girl, told her about your club and your invitation, and we'll come this Friday."

"Great! I'll put you down on my VIP list: Maura Westover plus one. It'll just be one, right?"

"Yep, only one."

"Okay, it'll be good to see you again. Look me up when you get there." We hung up.

I heard Dab and Doc come in. They were in the kitchen when I got downstairs.

"What's up, fellas?" I asked.

"Just getting back from the greens," Doc said, rummaging in the refrigerator. "Want a brewski?"

"Yeah, hand me one," I responded.

"We had a foursome with Siramad and Angie," informed Dab. "Holliday almost got beat by Siramad. That girl's a natural golfer. This is only her third time playing with us." He pulled a bag of chips out of a cabinet.

"She didn't *almost* beat me," Doc protested. "I slacked up because I didn't want to annihilate her like you were trying to do." Doc handed me an MGD as he closed the fridge.

"Hey, just because she's a woman doesn't mean I'm gonna take it easy when she's competing against me," Dab enlightened. "That's not gonna make her better. Plus, if she beats me, I'll never hear the end of it."

"I'm glad my baby's not like that," Doc said with a grin, taking a swallow of his beer.

"She's not like that 'cause she ain't *yo'* baby," Dab corrected. "She's her *husband's* baby!"

"When she's with me-ski, she's *my* baby-ski!" Doc proclaimed. "What you been up to, Davey?"

"Just bored," I replied. "So where are the girls now?"

"They'll be over a little later after they change; we going to a movie this evening," Doc answered. "Bored, huh? That means you going through your phone book?"

"Naw, naw." Dab chuckled. "It probably means he's gonna concentrate on finding Miss Right again." They both laughed.

"Oh yeah," said Doc, "like he did a while ago with Honore." They were getting a kick out of my dilemma.

"Who's Miss Right this time?" asked Dab.

"I ain't looking for no Miss Right," I said.

"Hey, man, remember what I said," reminded Dab. "While you're waiting for Miss *Right*, have fun with the Miss *Wrong*." All three of us laughed at that one. Doc and I clinked bottles.

"Yeah, well, that's why I went through my phone book," I apprised. "To see which *wrong ones* I could conjure up."

"What you come up with?" asked Doc, passing around the bag of chips.

"The name of a girl with four stars," I shared, "but I can't put a face with the name."

"Hold it, hold it. Five stars is the best, right?" Dab asked.

"Right." I nodded.

"And she has four stars?" Dab went on.

"Yep." I nodded again.

"So what's the problem?" Dab queried. "You got a winner!"

"The problem is," I divulged, "I haven't seen or talked to her in two and a half years, and there has to be a reason for that. And not only can I not remember her face; I can't remember the reason either."

"Two and a half years!" Doc exclaimed. "Damn, you really *were* bored. Why did you go back so far?"

"Who knows," I said, nursing my beer. "Probably because I never got it"

"Uh-*huh*. So you never knocked it off," Doc rehashed, "you don't know what she looks like, and you can't remember why you stopped calling her?"

"Uh, yeah," I granted.

"So when are you supposed to see this mystery lady?" inquired Dab.

"She and a girlfriend are coming to the club this Friday."

"Oh. Well, handle it, brother," Doc said. "I'm gonna go get ready for the ladies." He left the kitchen to go upstairs.

"Tell me," Dab asked, sounding puzzled, "if you can't place her face and don't know why you stopped talking to her, how do you know you never hit it?"

"'Cause I can look at a name in my book and remember if I ever tapped it." I didn't want to tell him that besides stars, I also made black marks in my phone book next to the names of the ladies I had been intimate with.

"So even if you can't see the face," Dab summed up, "you can see the bush?"

I laughed. "That's about the size of it."

"Well," Dab said, as he also headed upstairs, "I guess you'll see the face Friday."

"And hopefully that's not all," I added.

⟋

Friday came. I was out on the enclosed patio of the club when Doc approached me with a smile on his face.

"Hey, man," he declared, "I think your four stars is here."

"Where?"

"She and her buddy were heading toward the back bar-ski. They may be going up to the VIP, 'cause I told them that's where you may be. They both have on black and are looking *good!*"

"C'mon and show me."

Doc and I weaved through the crowd toward the bar, greeting folks along the way. I saw some cuties that I knew who wanted me to stop and chat, but I indicated to them that I was on club business and would catch them a little later.

"There they are." Doc nodded to two attractive ladies in black. One had on a form-fitting black dress, and the other black satin pants that seemed to be painted on and a button-down black satin blouse. Both ensembles displayed voluptuous bodies. That's why a few guys had them surrounded as we approached.

I was surprised when I recognized the one in the satin outfit as Wanda Gurley, whom I had called the same night I called Maura. *Is that a clue?* I pondered. *Did I meet one via the other?* Wanda was looking very good—better than when I had last seen her over a year ago. She had long, dark sandy hair and light eyes. She was high yellow with a Creole look about her. Maura was the opposite. She was the prettiest chocolate lady I'd seen in a long time, with jet-black hair pulled back and parted down the middle, sparkling eyes, and a smile with deep dimples. I remembered the face vaguely now but still couldn't recall anything else.

"Excuse me, fellas," I said as I walked between the four guys around them to stand directly in front of Maura. "Hi, ladies." The guys looked at Doc and me with annoyed expressions.

"Davey Stein," Wanda said with a smile on her face. She gave me a hug.

"You're looking good, Wanda," I acknowledged.

"Hi, Davey," Maura greeted. She stepped toward me to get a hug too. "You're the one looking good." She smiled.

"Uh-uh," I objected, "it's you two. That's why you have a crowd around you." I laughed.

"Whazzup?" one of the guys asked.

"Oh, excuse us, guys," Maura said, addressing them. "This is the guy who invited me here; they are two of the guys who run this club."

"You guys having a good time?" I asked the four guys.

"Yeah, brother, we plan on having a great time," the guy who had spoken up said; they were smiling now.

"It was nice meeting y'all," Wanda said, dismissing them.

"Cool," the leader said as they turned away.

"Ladies, this is one of my partners and my roommate, Joseph," I introduced. "We all call him 'Doc.'"

"Yes, we spoke to him at the front," Wanda said, offering a hand to Doc. "I'm Wanda, and that's Maura." Doc shook hands with both.

"What are you drinking, ladies?" I asked.

"Can you find us a seat first?" Maura asked.

"What about up there?" Wanda indicated a couple of vacant tables in our dinner section.

"Those tables are reserved for folks having dinner until ten o'clock," informed Doc.

"Yeah," I said, looking at my watch and noticing that it was nine twenty-five, "but they stop serving dinner at nine thirty. So c'mon." I led them up the three steps to our slightly elevated dinner section, which was between the entrance and the bar. We sat at a table for four near the brass railing that enclosed the area. A waitress came over with menus in hand.

"Hi Doc, Davey." She smiled. "You guys having dinner?"

"Hey, Heather," we both responded. I then said, "No, we're just going to have some drinks. What are you drinking, ladies?"

"Two Hpnotiqs," Maura said, "and can we look at one of your menus?"

"Sure." Heather handed them one. "Davey—cuba libre? Doc—Hennessey and Coke?"

"You got it," I confirmed.

Doc had been flirting with Wanda ever since I introduced them. Now he rose and said, "Actually I have a drink waiting for me at our VIP table. I'm gonna holler at you guys a little later." He looked at me, shook his head, and then gave me a thumbs-up as he left the area.

"What did you say to him?" I asked Wanda.

"I just told him that I was interested in you," she replied with a coy smile. Maura laughed as she was perusing the menu.

"Wha'chu talkin' 'bout, Wanda?" I gave her my best "Arnold" look.

Wanda smiled. "Talkin' 'bout you, Davey."

"Uh, by the way, I didn't know you two knew each other," I said, changing the subject. Then I thought, *Did I?*

"Actually, we just met recently," Wanda said.

"Yeah, I moved into her complex several months ago," Maura elaborated, "and we'd see each other in the area—in the laundry room, the exercise room, the game room—so we introduced ourselves about a month ago."

"And we started hanging out," Wanda added.

Heather brought our drinks.

"Davey, I'd like to order something to snack on," Maura requested.

"Go ahead," I okayed offhandedly, thinking about what Wanda had told Doc. *What's going on here?* Both ladies ordered an appetizer and an entrée from Heather.

I started getting that "played" feeling. *I'm sure they know that I called them both on the same night,* I mused, *and Wanda probably told Maura that I attempted to invite myself over to her place that same night before I called Maura. So what's their plan—to gorge me? Or did Wanda share my prowess in bed with Maura and they are interested in a ménage à trois? Now, that would be nice. But let me see which way the wind blows.*

"You know, that's a strange coincidence," I began, squeezing the lime's juice into my drink. "I called both you ladies the same night, not knowing you knew each other."

"Yes," agreed Maura, "that was strange. In fact, after I got off the phone with you, I called Wanda back and we laughed about it."

"Oh, you guys got a laugh out of it, huh?"

"Yeah, we did," Wanda affirmed, "and then I told her about you."

"Uh, told her about me?"

Maura smiled. "Yes, yes, yes. Wanda told me how good you were in bed and that you have a very talented mouth." They high-fived each other across the table.

"Oh, she did, did she?"

"And I told her that I never got a chance to find out how talented you were," Maura continued, "because of my situation."

"Uh, your 'situation'? Uh … what, uh, 'situation'?"

"You remember," Maura scoffed.

"Oh, oh, yeah," I lied, hoping she would continue.

"That crazy Mario," she continued. "He figured since our names were similar that we were meant to be together forever."

"Yeah, that, uh, crazy Mario," said I, trying to remember.

"He acted a fool at the Warehouse that night," she reminisced. "Remember?"

The Warehouse. A spark was trying to light. *The Warehouse.* Some air hit the spark. *The Warehouse?* The spark became a flame. *The Warehouse!* The flame became a roaring fire! *Oh yeah, the Warehouse!* I remembered.

Before we started promoting Rendezvous, Doc, Dab, Doug, and I were promoting a spot called the Greenhouse on Fridays in the Mid-Wilshire area. I was at a house party one Saturday and met Maura. She was with her boyfriend. I had invited them both to the club, though I had intended to invite only Maura, not the guy. He went to the bathroom, and she slipped me her number. I called her, and we talked a long while, and she told me that her boyfriend, Mario, was very, very jealous and was abusive too. She said that she'd tried many times to break up with him, but he wouldn't let her go.

She came to the club once with a girlfriend, but Mario showed up and caused a scene. I stopped calling her for a couple of weeks. Finally she agreed to go out with me one day when Mario was supposedly out of town. We went to the Warehouse—a seafood restaurant in the marina. When we were leaving, there was Mario out front, refusing to let the valet pull my car up. He was cursing, screaming, and threatening. He had a couple of guys with him.

The restaurant called the cops on him, and they took the three of them away. Mario hollered out, as they were throwing him in the squad car, that he'd better not ever see my car at Maura's place. He even came by the Greenhouse with his boys to threaten me. Our security guys squelched that, but I kept an eye out for him when the fellas and I headed to our cars at the end of that night.

I had gotten a black belt in karate when I was in the military and stationed in Japan for two years, but I had never used that training in a fight, because I never got into fights. Like the old saying goes, "I'm a lover, not a fighter." But I always knew that, if need be, I could handle myself, even against three. However, I did not like drama, especially over a female. Now, if the female was a relative or someone I cared deeply for or was in danger, that was a different story. But fighting over a chick? Naw, that ain't me.

So after the two incidents, I stopped calling Maura. She called me a couple of times, but when I recognized her voice, I told her that I was busy and would call her back. I never did. I had seen her only three times, and the first two times were just brief glimpses in passing at the house party and the Greenhouse. She stopped calling.

"So how is Mario?" I inquired.

"Don't know," replied Maura. "I got a restraining order against him about a year and a half ago after he struck me again, but he kept calling me. Finally I moved several months ago to where I'm living now, and he hasn't bothered me or called me since. I guess he has a new project. I hope so anyway. I feel sorry for her." She laughed.

"So because of her ex-boyfriend," Wanda interjected, "she never got a chance to enjoy you like I did." Heather had brought their food by this time, and the ladies were digging in.

"And since Wanda bragged on you so much," Maura added, "we decided to come see you tonight."

"Just *see* me tonight, huh?"

"Well, that's up to you," Wanda stated. "We don't know your plans."

"Yeah," agreed Maura, "I know how '*busy*' you get."

That was a dig, I realized.

"Tonight," informed I, "I'm open to suggestions. What do you have in mind?"

Maura moved her chair closer to mine and put her hand on my

right thigh. Wanda then moved her chair closer to me and placed her hand on my left thigh.

"Have you ever been with two ladies?" Maura asked in my right ear, squeezing my thigh.

Actually, I had done it before, a couple of times, but they didn't need to know that.

"No, I never have," I told them.

"Well, tonight is your lucky night," Wanda whispered in my left ear, rubbing my thigh.

"Let's enjoy ourselves here tonight," Maura suggested in the other ear, "and then finish up over at Wanda's place."

I was in heaven. Here I was with two fine, sexy ladies, and I was *really* going to be with them a little later. The "played" feeling was rapidly being replaced by the "*laid*" feeling.

We went up to the VIP room after the ladies finished eating. They sat close to me on one of the leather couches and each of them had a leg draped over each of mine as we drank champagne and people-watched. They pulled me out on the dance floor when the deejay played "I'm a Flirt," and I became the meat in their sandwich. I couldn't wait to get to Wanda's.

I took them down to our VIP booth. Dab was there with his latest girl, Siramad, and Doc was with Angie, his married lady. Richard Butts, one of our partners, was also there with a lady. I introduced everyone to Maura and Wanda.

"We thought you had left," Dab said. "We looked for you."

"We were upstairs," I responded. "What's up?"

"We're going by Berrie's for breakfast when we leave here," Dab informed us. I had ridden to the club with him and Doc.

"No problem." I smiled. "I'm going to catch a ride with the ladies." They squeezed my leg underneath the table. They had been touchy-feely all night with me. So far I had been keeping my hands to myself, but I was planning on catching up on the touching and feeling later.

We stayed at the VIP booth until just before closing, drinking champagne, dancing, and telling jokes.

"Ladies, we should leave before it gets too crowded at the valet," I suggested.

"Oh, we lucked up and saw a car leaving as we drove up," Maura said, "so we parked on the street. But we are ready to go."

I beckoned for Heather to bring my bill. Since she had started serving us in the dinner section, I did all my subsequent ordering from her. We had a deal with the club owner that anything we ordered came with a deep discount. Even with that discount, my bill was higher than I had expected. But I shrugged and took care of it with a nice-sized tip for Heather. I still made money this night, *and* I was gon' get some honey too.

"All right, folks," I announced, rising with the ladies, "I'll catch you guys a little later."

"Yeah, we'll see you when we see you," Doc said, giving me an all-knowing wink.

I walked out to the car with a lady on each arm. All three of us were feeling good from the champagne and the innuendo. They directed me around the corner to Wanda's vehicle. I leaned up against it with an arm around both ladies and pulled them up against me. I squeezed each plump ass, and they both kissed me on a cheek.

"You, uh, have a nice evening, Davey," Wanda said as she kissed my left cheek.

"I'm about to," I responded, squeezing again.

"Oh yeah?" Maura asked. "With whom?"

"With you two," I replied with a chuckle.

"Guess again," said Wanda.

"I don't think so," said Maura.

"Hmm, so what's *really* going on?" I asked, taking my hand off their butts.

"Davey, Davey, Davey," Maura began. "Let me share something with you. Mario was the continuation of a string of bad relationships that I endured. In fact, he was the worst, with his punches, pushes, and name-calling. Toward the end of him, I reached out to you. I know you didn't know this then, but when I called you after the incidents at the restaurant and your club, I was calling because you seemed so nice and I wanted to be comforted by you. But you told me that you were busy and would call me back. And you never did. Davey, you never *did!* I resented you after that. I resented men, period." Maura extricated herself from my hold, as did Wanda, and they stood in front of me on that side street, holding each other, looking at me.

"And Davey," Wanda added, "I finally had enough of you men thinking that after taking me out a couple of times that my body became yours and y'all could just call and come by whenever the whim hit you to hit *it.*"

"After I moved into Wanda's complex," Maura continued, "and we met and talked about relationships and men, I told her that I had gone in an entirely different direction about a year ago and how satisfying and beautiful it was. She told me that she wanted to try it." They hugged each other, looking at me. And then Wanda took Maura's face in her hands and kissed her deeply and passionately. I heard Maura whimper as Wanda's hand squeezed her plump butt. And I must admit, watching those two sexy ladies kissing really turned me the hell on!

"So when you called us both the same night," Wanda said after the kiss, "it reinforced my feelings about how doggish you men are."

"Yep," Maura agreed. "Let's go, baby. It's you and me tonight." She affectionately slapped Wanda's butt.

Maura got in on the passenger side, and Wanda walked around to the driver's side. I just stood there with my mouth open, saying nothing, feeling foolish, and imagining these two sexy pretty ladies doing each other.

"So we decided to come here tonight," Wanda said, "to eat, drink, and have a good time at your expense, and then go home together. Just us two." She started the car and powered down the passenger window. "And Davey," she added as she leaned over Maura to look out the opened window at me, "remember what I said the other night?" She reached out and fondled Maura's left breast. "Well, it's the *new* Wanda, and tonight will be the first time for Maura and me together, because tonight marks the end of *a month!*"

They were both laughing as she burned rubber, taking off down the street.

Damn shame! I thought. After a thought, I yelled at them, "Well, at least send me some pictures!"

SATURDAY KNIGHT'S SPECIAL

ALTHOUGH THE WEATHER WAS BASICALLY MELLOW ALL YEAR LONG in LA, we still liked to get out more in the warmer months in sunny Southern California. Memorial Day weekend was usually the kickoff for me. Spring was a nice season, but summer was my favorite time of the year. And that coincided with my admiration for the female figure.

Those bodies needed less and less clothing to cover them starting with the last weekend in May. You see, I am a connoisseur of the female body. As far as I am concerned, that is the greatest thing known to man. The female body—what a creation when it's put together just right, with the right equipment in the right proportions, strategically placed in the right areas. What a machine!

Saturday Knight was a machine that was made to drive—drive a man crazy.

That's right, Saturday Knight. That was her name. She was about five feet, six inches tall; 35-23-37 were the rest of her measurements. She was brown-skinned, with soft, curly sandy locks; high cheekbones; luscious lips; a pretty smile; and big, pretty dark brown eyes. She had one of the smallest waists I'd ever seen on a woman with hips like hers. She was like an angel. But angels sometimes have secrets.

I met her at a birthday party. I was there with my roomies, Dab and Doc. She was with some friends also. We had a nice conversation out on the balcony as the party was going on. I noted her sweet, demure personality. She revealed to me that she was a librarian at the Inglewood Library over behind city hall. That was all the information I needed.

A couple of weeks after meeting her, I was visiting a member of my pinochle crew, Trace Von Tyler, whose law office was in the city hall building in Inglewood. Parking in downtown Inglewood, which consisted of only a few blocks, was a trip. So since my buddy's law firm validated, I parked in the public lot, and after shooting the breeze with him and getting my ticket stamped, I walked around the block to the library.

I surprised Saturday by showing up, but it delighted her, I saw. I took her to lunch. We had a good time. She hadn't given me her number at the party, but this time she did. After that day, we talked a lot by phone. She lived with her mother and father and was an only child.

During our many telephone conversations, I found out that she didn't get along well with her mother, who wanted her to get her own place, but adored her father, who babied his little girl. Sometimes we would talk for hours on the phone about it. She cried sometimes because she felt that she was being pulled in two different directions. I told her that maybe she *should* find her own place. That was out of the question to her. She felt safe at home, and her folks didn't charge rent.

I ran into her at the Speakeasy one Friday night. She was there with a couple of girlfriends. As it got later, she was ready to go, but her friends balked. Saturday asked me whether I would take her home, and I agreed.

You see, I was taking my time with this lady. She seemed to be so delicate, and that made me want her badly, but I didn't want to scare her off by coming on too strong. I deemed her a lady worthy of a slow, gentlemanly approach. In fact, I never mentioned her to my best friends, Dab and Doc. I decided to make her my secret girl, my take-it-slow lady.

We sat outside her house talking for a while after I took her home, and then just before she exited the car, we kissed. Whenever I think of the softest, sweetest lips I've ever kissed, I think of Saturday

Knight's lips. Her lips were buttery soft, full, moist, and giving. I didn't want to stop kissing them. They made me want to come.

"You know I'm turned on by you," I told her. "I want you."

"I'll talk to you tomorrow, Davey," she said with a hand on my thigh.

I knew that was it. I was going to get some of that the next day, no doubt.

Early the next morning, I called her, and she suggested that we should go to brunch. I picked her up and took her to the marina. We ate at TGI Fridays.

"What do you want to do now?" I asked.

"I want to be alone with you," she admitted, "but I don't want to go to your place, because you have roommates."

"Well, let's find a motel," suggested I. She nodded.

I found one in the marina. I didn't want to take her to the Snooty Fox or the Baldwin Hills Motel, which were two of the popular hourly motels near where I lived. The thing is, I was prone to run into someone I knew at those places.

On a Friday or Saturday night after the clubs closed, cars would be lined up at the check-in window, trying to get a room for anywhere from one to four hours at the Baldwin Hills location. The women would wait in the car while the guys paid for the room. The staff would knock on the door when the time was up. I mean, uh … that's, uh … that's what I heard. I called them no-tell motels.

Anyway, back to Ms. Knight.

After entering the motel room in the marina, we sat on the bed for a moment and looked at each other. I wanted to taste those lips again. I reached for her and pulled her close. As we were kissing, my hand was inching its way up her thigh under her skirt. Just as I started rubbing her crotch, she pushed me away.

"Stop," she said softly.

I did.

We sat there holding hands for a few minutes, and then she leaned her face toward mine, and we began kissing again, very passionately. My hand worked its way back under her skirt.

"Stop," she said again.

This time I sat back and looked at her. "What's wrong?"

"Nothing," she said. "Uh, maybe this was a bad idea. We should leave."

"Leave?"

"Yes, I want to go home."

"Cool." I was calm. "Let's go." *I just wasted money on this room*, I realized. This place didn't charge by the hour like the "no-tell motels" in the hood.

I parked around the corner from her house, and we started kissing passionately. I wanted to turn around and head back to that motel. I had kept the room key in my pocket, just in case. Hell, it was paid for. She was moaning as I kissed her and began tweaking her nipples.

"Please stop," she moaned.

I did, and I drove around the corner to her house, frustrated.

"I'll call you later," she promised as I let her out.

She did. She called and apologized for her behavior. She suggested that we get together the next weekend.

The next day was volleyball day. When the weather was nice, a group of us met on Sunday mornings just before noon at Cheviott Hills-Rancho Park on Motor near Pico, right across the street from Twentieth Century Fox movie studios.

This had been an ongoing event for a few years now, and we had a great following of men and women: my roommates, Dab and Doc; my college buddies, Claude, Doug, and Denn; my Tuesday-night pinochle crew; and a variety of other female and male friends we partied with. We would also invite new females we met at our events or wherever who were athletically inclined or who just wanted to come and watch.

We usually kicked it off the Sunday after Memorial Day and did it all summer and fall, while the weather was nice. We made it a picnic affair. Folks brought coolers filled with drinks and snacks. I always had the net, poles, and balls in the trunk of my car. Consequently, I was usually the first one out there, because I had to set up the area.

We used a flat area just outside of the softball diamonds. Sometimes we even played a little softball, too, depending on the crowd.

We played six on a team in volleyball and tried to make sure that we had equal numbers of females on the contending teams. When a team lost, the person who had the next game could pick from the losers and the other folks who were sitting around on blankets and chairs playing bid whist or dominoes.

It was great fun. There were a few ladies in the group who could hold their own on the volleyball court. And they looked good too!

On this day in particular, I was playing bid whist, with Doc as my partner, against Denn Elliott and Dab. Denn was one of the coolest brothers I knew. He had been that way in college too. He had a way with the women, and he was a good volleyball player and moved well on the court. He hailed from the Midwest, drove a Cadillac Seville, and lived in the Jungle. Denn was good at catching the CODs.

The Jungle was an area of LA a person didn't want to get caught in after dark. Hell, a person didn't want to get caught there during the day if he or she looked out of place. But when it was first built, it was said to be the model for like developments across the whole country.

It was blocks and blocks of apartment buildings that were two-story architectural masterpieces when they were conceived. They each had an inner court with a swimming pool, and some had Jacuzzis. Palm trees were out front and in the courtyard areas. Exotic plants like birds of paradise were abundant out front and in the courtyards also. The landscapes were remarkable.

Back in the early '70s, middle-class Blacks—doctors, lawyers, teachers, and folks in the entertainment industry—and middle-class Whites were residents of the Jungle.

It wasn't called the Jungle back then, of course. It was the lower part of the Baldwin Hills area. Even on maps today it's still shown as Baldwin Hills. But more lower-class Blacks and, later, Mexicans, started moving in, and crime became commonplace, with helicopters flying around every night, shining their searchlights, and the Black doctors, Black lawyers, and Whites started moving out to View Park, Ladera Heights, the Dons, and Beverly Hills. That's when it became known as the Jungle. The movie *Training Day*, starring Denzel Washington, later depicted it to a T.

Denn moved there just before it started getting bad. In fact, a popular young sitcom TV star and his mother lived in the same complex as Denn, before the star got even more popular.

"Fellas, I met this bad babe a few weeks ago." Denn was shuffling the cards as he spoke.

"What's so bad about her?" Dab asked.

"She's a freak, man." Denn grinned. "A stone freak."

"Freaky how?" Dab fished.

"Sexy freaky," Denn shared. "And I found out accidentally."

"Accidentally?" Doc asked.

"Yeah," Denn went on, "I had her at my crib one day after meeting her at the Red Onion in the Marina. We were kissing—man, she has the softest lips I've ever kissed."

For some reason, my ears perked up.

Denn continued. "Then she told me to stop. I got up, went into the kitchen had a drink of water and came back and sat back down next to her. I was pissed. I hate it when these chicks do that shit. So I sat back down on the couch, and she asked what was the matter. I didn't say anything; I just started kissing her again. I could tell she was feeling it, but she said 'stop' again.

"I went off. I said, 'Shut up, bitch!' She said, 'Don't call me that,' but I heard something in her voice that clued me in that she was getting turned on. So I kept it up. 'Fuck you, bitch, just shut the fuck up and kiss me.' She started kissing my face and reaching for my crotch area, still asking me not to call her that. I called her a bitch, a ho, a cunt—anything I could think of—and she got even hotter. I stood up in front of her and told the heifer to suck my dick. She was all over that mug, acting like she wanted to swallow the whole thing. Best blowjob I ever had. Sweet lips.

"Man, I fucked her in every hole she had, cussing her out the whole time. The more I cussed and called her names, the hotter and wetter she got. That babe comes over two times a week now. And each time, I have to do the same thing to jump-start her ass. And get this: the jive chick is a librarian." He laughed as he finished.

I couldn't believe what I was hearing. "What's her name?" I asked, not wanting to hear the answer.

"Saturday." He laughed.

"Saturday?" Dab chuckled. "What a fucking name. Why do Black folks do that to their kids? Saturday. What's her last name, Afternoon? Saturday Afternoon?" He laughed.

"Actually, it's Knight, with a *K*," corrected Denn. "Saturday Knight." The three of them roared.

"Give me a break," Dab scoffed.

"What's wrong, Davey-ski?" Doc probed, noticing that I wasn't laughing.

"Uh, nothing," I said evasively. "Just a twinge of pain from when I dived for the ball earlier. It'll go away." I didn't want Doc and Dab to know that I knew the "sexy freaky" lady.

I called Saturday the next day. We made plans to go to the movies Thursday night. After the feature, we had drinks at a little spot on Wilshire near LaCienega. I asked her how things were at home. Her mom was really being an asshole, she informed me, but her dad was there for her. She enjoyed the quiet times she had with him when her mother was at one of her school board meetings.

I told her maybe she just didn't understand her mother. She said her mother didn't understand her. Her mother thought that at twenty-eight she should want to be in her own place instead of under her and her father's roof. Saturday felt that as an only child, her mom should understand how hard that was for her to do. Her father understood, she shared, but her mother did not.

Quiet as it was kept, I didn't understand either. Neither could I understand how this quiet, demure, sensitive lady could be the same "freak" that Denn was seeing.

I parked around the corner from her house. She slid over and put her head on my shoulder. I looked at her luscious lips and wondered whether I should kiss them now that I knew what she was doing with them.

She reached up and kissed me. For some reason, it felt strange. I mean, the whole evening I had been looking at her as though she was a different person now that I knew about her secret side. She just didn't appear to be the girl Denn had told us about. I dropped her off in front of her house.

The next Sunday, Denn was at it again. "Last night was Saturday's Knight," he giggled. "What I like is I don't have to take her anywhere now. She just comes over, drinks a beer with me, and it's on like popcorn."

He said she liked for him to order her to do what she wanted to do anyway. She wanted him to call her names, to tell her graphically what he wanted her to do with her mouth, with her pussy, and with her ass. He said she loved it, that she would get wetter than any woman he'd ever been with, that she was insatiable, that she was the freak of the week.

I decided to let Denn know that I knew her too. I could tell that she was just another fuck to him—that he didn't mind sharing. He used to say that we shared these ladies anyway, whether we knew it or not.

I pulled him aside between volleyball games and told him. But I added that she always put up the stop sign if I attempted to go past the kissing stage. I admitted to Denn that Saturday always gave signs that she wanted to go further, like the time at the motel, but that I would back off if she resisted a little. Denn told me that "resisting" was part of her foreplay. She wanted to appear to be forced.

I shrugged and changed the subject. I liked Saturday and didn't want to hear or believe what Denn was implying.

The next two Sundays, when the group met for our weekly volleyball games at the park, Denn told Doc, Dab, and me about the latest episodes with Saturday. Sometimes she'd come by late without calling first, and he'd had to break her of *that* habit.

Finally the thought of the sexy, attractive librarian being a freak wore me down. Doc and Dab were going out of town for a golfing event for a few days, and I decided I would call Saturday and ask her to come by for a drink. I knew her favorite drink was sex on the beach. Denn had instructed me on how to handle it if I ever wanted to get with her: "All you gotta to do is push her to the floor, man. Call her a bitch; order the bitch to take your dick out and suck it," he counseled. "She'll start crying and ask you not to call her a bitch, but it's an act; eventually she'll say 'Yes, honey' over and over again as she does anything and everything you want her to do with gusto. But don't let up, man; stay stern, and definitely keep calling her *bitch* or *ho* or whatever term you wanna use."

I didn't tell Denn that I was going to invite Saturday over and put his advice to the test while my roomies were going to be hanging out late at Lil J's.

She looked so good when I opened the door to let her in that Wednesday night—so innocent, demure, and pure. *Maybe there is another librarian named Saturday Knight out there*, I thought. I wanted to ask her if she knew a guy named Denn but thought better of it.

I poured her a sex on the beach from the ready-made mix I had picked up on the way home at the Liquor Bank. I showed her around, engaging in small talk. We ended up in my bedroom. After a while, we were kissing. My hands were on her buttocks, and I squeezed them. She moaned and started kissing me harder. I pushed her away, looking as mean as I could.

"All right, bitch, it's time to get on your knees!" I growled.

"W-w-what!" Her eyes got wide with surprise.

"I said *get* on your fucking knees, bitch!" I repeated in my sternest tone, glowering at her. Then I pushed her to the floor.

"Don't call me *that*!" she wailed, just as Denn had said she would.

"Shut up, bitch!" I continued, half-heartedly. "Unzip my pants, bitch, and suck my fucking dick … bitch!"

"*Please* don't call me that!" she pleaded tearfully as she writhed on the floor, again as Denn had predicted. "Don't *make* me do it!"

"Why not, bitch?" I shouted, trying to remain cold but finding it hard to do so. "You are a bitch and a ho, ain't you … bitch!"

"Don't call me 'bitch'; don't make me do it!" she cried, looking up at me with wet eyes.

I gave in. My heart wasn't in it. I couldn't go through with it.

"I … I'm sorry, baby," I apologized, helping her to her feet, kissing her tears away, and calming her down. "I was just playing. I, uh, I don't know what, uh, came over me. I'm so sorry."

She had a strange look on her face as she accepted my apologies. She looked bewildered, lost. Abruptly she said she had to go. It was almost nine o'clock. I walked her to her car and watched her drive off hurriedly with squealing tires as my conscience started beating up on me.

How could I do such a thing? Denn had to be making that shit up, I decided. *Or that had to be a different librarian named Saturday.*

"Man, I ain't *never* seen Saturday as hot as she was when she came by *this* week," Denn informed us that next Sunday at the park. "It was like she was high on something."

"She just came by?"

"Yeah, I really gotta break her of that shit. I might have some other chick over. Hmm, I wonder if she would—"

"Uh, what day was it?" I interrupted, out of curiosity.

"It was Wednesday night about nine o'clock," Denn said. "She walked in the door *hot.* She just dropped to the floor as soon as the door closed and gave me a blowjob to beat all blowjobs, and then we made out all night in every room. I didn't even have to call her any names! But I did anyway, just in case. Wore me the hell *out!* Davey, man, you oughta get some of that!"

"Uh, no thanks, Denn." I smiled. "I think, uh, I think Saturday is yo' Knight. I'll stick to the other days of the week."

WHY MUST I CHASE DA CAT?

ONE DAY IT HIT ME.

I've got to grow up! I can't chase women with Doc and Dab forever. I've got to find me a good woman to settle down with, and I've got to do it soon. These are my prime catching years. I'm only in my midthirties; I can still approach ladies in their midtwenties on up and not be considered a dirty old man. After a while, I won't be able to do that. I mean, I'll still do it—if I'm not married—because I like ladies in their midtwenties on up. I'll just be a dirty old man doing it. If it comes to that, I can live with it.

But right now, I should take a step back, look at the ladies I know, and pick a good one to get to know better and possibly get serious about. Or, if none of them do it for me, I need to be on the lookout for one that does. It's time to get serious.

Yep, one day I had those thoughts. And I acted on them.

You see, my life has always been a series of relationships—usually six-month relationships. None lasted much longer than that. But in between those relationships, sometimes I became lonely. Even when I hung out with Doc and Dab or Denn and some of my other running buddies, I still felt pangs of loneliness at times.

Everyone thinks that bachelors who live exciting lives and who are always out there being active, giving parties, and showing up at other hot events around town are totally happy.

Not true.

Sometimes they're the loneliest guys in the world. They disguise their loneliness as "freedom." They tell everyone—and themselves—that as long as they are *free* to come and go as they please, they're happy.

But it's a lie.

Deep down, most folks crave companionship and crave someone to share their life with—someone to confide in, someone just to hold in the middle of the night and early in the morning, and someone to look forward to coming home to.

Anyway, I was having these feelings one day. It probably had something to do with the fact that Dab, Doc, and I had just gotten back from Doug's—our ex-roommate's—wedding to his soul mate, Copper, in Atlanta.

I was sitting in my room, listening to a cassette I had made a year or so earlier, titled *Love Songs for My Soul Mate*, which was inspired by Doug's cassette that he told me he'd made years ago. As I listened, I thought about the ladies I'd dated. I thought about the ones who could have made good wives and the past relationships that had potential.

The names went through my head like a roll call: *Coreen Charles, Minnie Handley, Vanessa Jamison, Bertha Butler, Honore James, Renee Chapman, Evelyn Underwood …*

All of them brought forth some good memories, but the one who elicited the most was Ms. James. Honore James.

I prided myself in dealing with classy ladies, but Honore had a classiness about her that made her stand out from the day I first met her at that First Fridays event. Not to mention that fabulous booty and face.

She wore a short haircut that made her look like a slightly darker version of Halle Berry. Plus she was a Libra, which was the sign that elicited the most excitement out of me. That's why most of the ladies I was drawn toward were Libras, although I liked the other two air signs, Gemini and Aquarius too. And Sagittarians had a thing about them.

But back to the subject.

Honore and I had broken up months earlier because she said

that she was looking for something serious and she felt that I wasn't ready for that. She felt that I had ladies at my beck and call, and that I was doing too much becking and calling. She claimed that I ran the streets way too much with the fellas and that I wasn't ready to spend "quality time" with her.

And, damn it, she was right—at the time. But *that* time had passed, I had convinced myself. Now I had to convince her that I had changed. Because now it was different. *I* was different.

This soul-searching I was doing led me to believe that I was ready to settle down with a good woman and be a good man. I had to show Honore that I wasn't the same guy I had been several months earlier. That was way before I had gone to Doug's wedding. Way before I had seen how happy and relaxed he was by just being near Copper.

He was my old college buddy. He, Denn, and I used to run the streets of DC and LA together before I met Dab and Doc. I was the best man at his wedding. I had always thought I would get married before he did. I couldn't let him get away with that!

He married the girl I would've married had I met her first. Copper was a dream, and she, too, was a Libra. In fact, Honore reminded me of her in so many ways. *That seals it. Honore must be the one picked for me to settle down with.*

All right, I mused, *first I've got to make sure she's not involved with anyone. And if she is, I need to nix it.*

The fact is, she had been the hardest one to let go. But it had gotten close to the six-month threshold, and my inner clock had gotten antsy.

I also had this other thing. When I was tired of being with a lady, I would do things to make *her* want to break up with me. I always wanted to make it appear that splitting up was my fault but was the lady's idea. That way, I presumed, it would be easier for the lady to leave me alone, because she would think *she* had broken up with me.

It always worked.

And then, after a while, the lady would get over it and become my friend again. And sometimes she would make herself available for booty calls.

Yep, I was always looking out for the feelings of others.

"So, Davey, why did you make it sound so urgent to see me?" Honore asked as we sat out on the balcony of her condo in Fox Hills overlooking the park across the street.

It was a nice sunny Saturday afternoon in June, late afternoon, close to five o'clock. The joggers were out, the tennis courts were busy, some picnickers were about, there was even a group playing volleyball in the sanded volleyball pit that my circle of friends occasionally used on Sundays after we stopped going to the park in Cheviott Hills.

"Because I've been doing a lot of soul-searching lately," I answered, "but first, let me ask you, have you found a new man yet?"

"There's a guy I met that I'm getting to know. Why?" We were drinking Martini & Rossi Asti Spumante and snacking on some seedless red grapes and string cheese, which she knew I liked.

"How serious are you about him?" We were sitting at her patio table.

"I'm just getting to know him. There's no seriousness about it yet. Now, why are you asking?" She seemed evasive, but I let it pass.

"Because I haven't been with *one* lady since you and I stopped seeing each other." Actually I had been with three other ladies since we'd stopped seeing each other, so that statement was not really a lie.

"I find that hard to believe."

"Believe it; I haven't been with *one!*" I reiterated. "But, like I said, I've been doing some soul-searching, and I realize that running these streets is not where it's at anymore."

"I could've told you that."

"Hey, I had to find out on my own, okay? And I did. It's getting old."

"So you're telling me that you're done chasing women and running the streets with Dan and Joe?"

"Uh huh. Dab and Doc are involved in relationships right now anyway." She liked calling Dab and Doc by their given names instead of their nicknames.

"So is that the only reason—because *they* are involved?"

"No! This has nothing to do with them. This is all about *me* and what *I* need … what *I* want."

"And what about the club?"

"The club is a business—a money-making business at that. It puts extra money in our pockets. I'm not giving that up, but it's strictly business."

"Uh huh."

"All I want to do right now is to be with one lady and see where it can go."

"Have you found her?"

"I'm looking at the lady I want to be with."

"Davey, if you'd said that a few months ago, we would've never broken up. I don't know if I can travel that road with you again. Plus I want to give this new guy a chance."

"Why would you want to take a chance on someone you don't know when you have someone tried and true who wants you?"

"You may be 'tried,' but I don't know about the 'true' part."

"That's what I want to show you."

"Why me now, Davey, huh? Why me?"

"Because of all the ladies I've ever dated, you're the one that still has a piece of my heart. Sometimes I lie in bed at night reminiscing about things we used to do." *Some of them were right here, in that bedroom back there! And on this patio!*

"That's sweet."

"And it's true. I just want you back in my life. I want to try to make you happy."

"I'm happy now, Davey."

"Happier."

"I don't know."

"What's so special about this new guy anyway?"

And just as she was about to tell me, the sucker called!

She got up and went inside as she talked to him on her cordless, giggling and acting like a schoolgirl, ignoring me. I got up and went to the railing and looked over at the people in the park three stories down.

This girl got the nerve to talk to another dude when I'm here? I ranted to myself. *I mean, I know we're just friends now, and this is a guy she's interested in, but damn! Another female would never distract me while I was in Honore's presence! I would keep all my focus on her!*

Then I saw the jogger across the street in the park. From a distance, I could tell her body was tight. The red-and-blue biker shorts and white T-shirt showed off her hourglass figure. And although her face was obscured by a blue baseball cap and sunglasses and distance, the reactions she was getting from the guys she passed made me think she had to be a beauty.

A part of me wanted to rush down there and attempt to meet her before she left the area. I don't think I need to tell you *which* part of me that was. But I decided to be cool. Honore was my target right now.

After about a half hour, she came back out on the balcony—just in time, because I was about to book.

"I'm sorry," she apologized. "That was Chauncey."

"Chauncey, huh? The new guy?"

"Yes. He wanted to know if I was busy tonight."

"Oh, he calls you on the day he wants to see you to ask you out? Why did he wait until the last minute?"

"Well, originally he was supposed to be out of town this weekend, but there was a change in plans."

"Oh, I see, 'a change in plans.' I wonder when that happened."

"Look, Davey, I know what you're trying to imply, but Chauncey isn't like that. Now, I like you, I really do; even after all these months, you still move me. But I don't know if I want to go backward."

I wondered if she was thinking about the way we had "moved" each other in that bedroom back there. We both were uninhibited when it came to sex, and we had done it everywhere in her condo— even out on this balcony and in our cars. And we'd done it all over the Mini-Mansion, too, when we were there without the fellas around.

"Sometimes you gotta take a step back to go forward," I philosophized.

"Aren't you the one who use to say, 'No steps backward'?"

"Uh, yeah, but … uh-ruh … sometimes when you, uh, misstep, a step *backward* puts you on the path that you're really supposed to be on—puts you back on track."

"Davey, let's both think this through. I have some things to do right now. Okay? But let's just be friends for now and see what happens."

"Honore, we will definitely always be friends. But I think we can be much more than that. Just give it some serious thought. I want a one-on-one quality relationship with the lady who moves me."

She moved me to her front door.

"I will think about it seriously," she relented. "We do have some good memories together."

She's gotta be thinking about the sex now, I figured.

"Who told you," I replied.

I leaned back against the door like I used to do when she was my girl and pulled her into my arms. She looked up at me with those pretty doe eyes, with her lips slightly parted. I kissed her passionately as my hands found her juicy butt and squeezed both cheeks. She moaned into my mouth.

"You still remember *Sexual Astrology*, huh?" she said as she pushed away, smiling. "That book nailed it with this Libra; I *do* get turned on by having my butt caressed. So you stop that."

I laughed. "I'll talk to you later. Now, don't you give him any tonight!"

"You don't have to worry about that; my period should be starting today or tomorrow."

"Uh huh," I replied, unconvinced. "Well, I know what you like to do when you're on your period."

"Davey," she said with a very serious look on her face, "I don't do everything with everybody. You and I had a special chemistry. Some stuff we did is just ours."

"I hear you, li'l girl." I was touched by that remark. "I'll talk to you later." I stood there in the hallway smiling at her until she closed the door and I heard the lock. *Yeah, I can get real serious about this woman again*, I reflected.

And then I dashed to the elevator.

Maybe that jogger is still in the park!

The elevator was taking too long. I hurried down the three flights of stairs. When I reached the entrance, I stood on the porch of Honore's building, looking across at the bustling park. I didn't see anyone in a red-and-blue outfit with a white top.

She may be still jogging and on the other side of the park, I thought. I crossed the street, unlocking the door of my black Lincoln LS with the remote. I retrieved a few flyers from the console with an eye glued to the jogging path, considering whether I should walk around it.

And then I saw her. She was walking tiredly, with hands on some great-looking hips, toward a bench under a cluster of trees a little deeper inside the park, where an adolescent was eating an orange.

It was at times like these that I really appreciated being a nightclub promoter. The flyers gave me a great way to approach strangers. As I walked over to the bench, I looked back up at Honore's unit to make sure she wasn't on her balcony.

"Excuse me, I don't mean to bother you," I said as I approached the jogger and the kid. "I just want to give you this invitation to our club over in Beverly Hills."

Now that I was in her presence, I saw that she looked like a beauty from afar, but up close she was a dream. She had the prettiest eyes I've ever seen. As she peered over her sunglasses at me, I saw they were hazel in color. She had long eyelashes, a sharp nose, high cheekbones, deep dimples, and a wide, sensuous mouth.

She glanced at my hand holding out the postcard-sized flyer but didn't reach out to take it. "What makes you think I like going to dance clubs?" she asked, trying to slow her breathing down, hands still on her hips. The kid, about ten years old, walked over to peek at the flyer in my hand.

I smiled. "Because you look like a lady who'd like to have fun in a conservative way."

She smiled back, which made her eyes sparkle. "Uh huh?"

"Plus our club offers more than just dancing," I added.

She took the flyer out of my hand. The young boy was trying to read it with her. "Oh, I've heard of Rendezvous," she acknowledged. "You're one of the guys who run it."

"Uh huh."

"Ah, you serve dinner with live jazz to begin the evening, huh?"

"Exactly. The deejay and dancing don't start until nine thirty."

"Great concept," she commended. "Which one of these names on the flyer is you?"

"The Davey Stein name. And you?"

"I'm Aura, and this is my son, Randolph."

"How you doing, Randolph?"

"I'm doing fine. How are you?" the kid responded in a friendly tone. I could see right off that he was a bright kid.

"I'm also doing fine, young man; I'm doing fine." I chuckled. "So, Aura, you think that you and a friend or two might want to check us out next Friday?"

"Well, I see you're going to have Cal Bennett there, so I might," she admitted. "I like him; I seen him perform at Hal's in Venice Beach a couple of times."

"Hal's huh? My friends and I go there sometimes on Sunday and Monday nights." I smiled. "Tell you what, here's a VIP card. Just show that at the door, and you and your guest will be admitted free."

"That's very kind of you, sir." She accepted it while reaching into a plastic bag to retrieve an orange.

"You want an orange?" Randolph asked.

"No, thank you," I replied. I didn't want to hang around too long and be seen by Honore. "So, Aura, I'll see you next Friday?"

"There's a good chance."

"So you'll be bringing your husband?"

"Don't have a husband."

"You'll be bringing your boyfriend?"

"Don't have a boyfriend."

"You'll be bringing …?"

"I'll be bringing a guest." She smiled her lovely, sparkling smile again.

"Well, I'll be looking forward to seeing you and your guest. Let me write my number on the back of that flyer in case you have any questions." She handed it back to me, and I pulled my ever-present pen out of my pocket and wrote down my number.

I wanted her number too, but I didn't want to ask for it with her son there. *If she comes to the club, I'll get it then*, I figured. "Randolph, it was nice meeting you, Aura it was a great pleasure meeting *you*. Have a good rest of the day."

I headed back to my car, trying to use the coolest of my strolls in case Aura was watching. It took me a couple of minutes to reach my ride. As I was about to get in it, I heard my name being called.

"Davey!" It sounded like Honore. I looked up at her balcony. She was leaning over it, looking down at me. "Davey!"

"Hey," I responded, waving. *Uh-oh!* I thought.

"Can you come back up, please?" she yelled down. Her voice sounded strange.

"Okay." I looked back discreetly as I started across the street. I saw Aura and Randolph walking in the opposite direction. *I hope she didn't hear Honore call my name.*

She buzzed me in. I was preparing my excuse as I rode up in the elevator. Her eyes were red and watery when she opened the door.

Damn, is she that upset about seeing me talking to Aura?

"Oh, Davey!" Honore wailed, throwing her arms around me.

"What's wrong, li'l girl?" I asked, ready to explain, holding her and patting her back. She had told me months earlier that she liked the comforting way I patted her back when I held her. And she liked me calling her "li'l girl."

"This woman called me!" she sobbed.

"W-w-what?" I was confused.

"Sh-she c-ca-called me, and sh-she t-t-told me to l-l-leave her man alone!" she said convulsively.

"What woman?" I asked, wondering which one of the women I knew would do that.

"C-C-Chauncey's woman!" she wailed.

"What!"

"*C-Chauncey's* woman!" she repeated emphatically as she held me tighter.

"What happened? What did she say?" I asked as I led her to her cream-colored leather sofa. We sat down.

"Sh-she said t-to leav-leave her man alone," she related, trying to control her sobs, "and that h-he was-wasn't going anywhere to-to-tonight."

I smiled inwardly. *I knew something was up with that last-minute date.* "Oh, li'l girl, I'm sorry," I said.

"A-a-and I heard him in th-the back-background t-t-tell-telling her th-that I-I-I wouldn't le-leave him alone," she continued, building up to more sobs, "and th-that he-he-he was just seeing me to-to-tonight to-to tell me th-that it was o-o-o-o-*ver!*" Racking sobs came gushing out as her body convulsed.

I just sat there holding her, stroking her arms. One thing about my breakups is that there was never any other lady caught up in them. I didn't deal with crazy ladies. I'd never had one of my ladies call another of my ladies talking shit. Uh-uh. No way! I don't like drama like that in my life. When I broke up with someone, it was just between her and me, no one else.

Honore laid her head in my lap. "Davey, you don't have to go, do you?" She asked. She was a little schoolgirl again.

"Uh, no, I don't have to go."

"Will you stay with me?"

"I'll stay with you."

"I was going to make spaghetti and a salad and garlic bread for that C-Chauncey. The stuff is already laid out in the kitchen."

"Don't worry; I will make it for us."

"You *will*?"

"Yes. No problem." I slid down to the end of the couch, gently lifted her head, and replaced my lap with the pillow. "You just lie here and leave everything to me."

"Okay. I-I just can't believe this day. I couldn't believe I was getting a call like that from another female. This ain't *The Jerry Springer Show!*" She began crying anew.

I knelt and kissed her on the forehead. "It's gonna be all right, li'l girl; it's gonna be all right."

"I'm glad you were here, Davey. I saw your car still out there and was gonna come find you," she said with her eyes closed.

I patted her back as I stood to go into the kitchen. She looked good. She had no makeup on her tear-stained face and was still one of the most gorgeous ladies I'd ever dated. Her sexy figure just oozed out of her around-the-house-wear—her cutoff jeans and sleeveless T-shirt. Sexy and beautiful—a great combination.

I went into the kitchen and got started on the food. I boiled the pasta; seasoned the ground turkey with some black pepper, seasoning salt, oregano, and onions; and cut up some Hillshire Farm smoked turkey sausage also. I cooked it all over a medium flame. A jar of Ragù got heated up as I prepared a spinach-and-lettuce salad to which I added some chopped pecans, onions, tomatoes, and sliced seedless grapes. As everything was finishing up, I put the garlic bread in the oven. She always kept bottles of wine around. *Ah ha, Lambrusco, which I love with Italian food.* I opened it and poured a little into the sauce. It started smelling good in there.

I looked around for something good to eat for dessert. Then I realized that dessert was lying on the couch.

Oops, her period is coming on!

I looked around for something good to eat for dessert. A pint of Häagen-Dazs strawberry and a pint of butter pecan were staring me in the face when I opened her freezer. *That'll have to do.*

I arranged the dining-room table and woke Honore, who had dozed off. I led her to the table and served us both as she sat there. Her sadness gave her a hearty appetite. She ate two helpings of spaghetti and bread with her salad, complimenting me on everything. I must admit, it was good. We each had two glasses of wine. She took her third glass into the bedroom, telling me she was going to lie down and asking me not to leave.

Hell, I'm not going anywhere! The door has opened for me to ease back in.

I began cleaning up the dining room and kitchen as fast as I could. I wanted to hurry up and ease on into that bedroom.

As the evening wore on, she calmed down considerably. We talked a little while we were eating. I wanted to know why the Chauncey situation bothered her so much, since she had said earlier that she was just getting to know this guy.

She admitted that she had been downplaying it earlier; she had been seeing him for a couple of months. But there had been a few other cancelled dates before, which had alerted her to be cautious. That was why the earlier call from the woman had upset her so much.

I finished cleaning up. Honore was propped up in bed with the TV turned down low. I stood there in the doorway of her very feminine bedroom, admiring her. She looked at me, smiled, and patted the space next to her.

"Come here, you," she said seductively.

Luckily there was no period yet. There was no question mark, either, because she knew it would start the next day with the help of my deep penetrations. There was just an exclamation point. In fact, there were a couple. I provided the bulk of the punctuation.

We were all over each other in that bed. She had always been very passionate and energetic when we had sex, but we made *love* this night. I'm here to tell you, sex is better when you're making love.

We woke up about four in the morning and went at it again. I was kissing her eyelids as I slowly drove into her soft, smooth, hot, moist opening, and she was cooing to me, pulling me deeper inside her, and I was thinking, *Yeah, this is her. This is the lady I want to be with. This is the body I want lying next to me, under me, on top of me. Honore, Honore. Yep, this is her. This is her. This is … Damn, that Aura is one fine babe! She has a helluva body, and the prettiest eyes. I wonder if she's coming to the club next Friday.*

⟶

The next morning, Honore went to church. She asked me to go with her. I declined, telling her that it would take too long for me to go home, shower and change clothes, and then come back over.

I had gone to her church with her once before several months ago, and I liked Agape. But my roomies had mentioned meeting my pinochle crew—a group of guys that I had played cards with once a week for the past ten years—over at Shanghai Red in the marina for brunch.

It was close to eleven when I got to the Mini-Mansion. Doc and Dab apparently had already left for the marina. Everyone wanted to get there before the after-church crowd arrived. I took a quick shower, changed, and jumped back into my ride.

After the valet scooped up Black Beauty—that's what I called my Lincoln LS—I found the fellas sitting at a big circular table inside the main dining area. Doc and Dab were there, along with one of our partners at Rendezvous, Richard "Rich" Butts, and the pinochle crew: Darren "Jenks" Jenkins, a gynecologist; Lance Phelps, a real estate entrepreneur; Guy Tell, Lance's play brother and business partner; Trace Von Tyler, a corporate attorney; Conrad "Connie" Carver, a systems engineer; and Daniel "Big Dan" Preston, an electronics engineer. Big Dan was six feet, seven inches tall. Dab—Daniel Dabineau—was nine inches shorter, but no one dared called him "Li'l Dan."

I greeted everyone, and after the waitress brought my mimosa, I got in line and made my selections from all the delicacies that were on display in the different rooms. It was quite an array. I started out light and came back to the table with two plates, a big pecan waffle on one and an omelet stuffed with crab, shrimp, cheese, and a variety of veggies on the other. The group was already enjoying their plates and discussing our favorite subject—women.

"So, fellas," I asked in between bites, "who wants my little black book?"

Connie spoke up first, shaking his head. "Uh-uh, I don't want those chicks calling me, cursing me out for something *you* did."

Everyone laughed.

"I heard that," Big Dan cosigned.

"Why you giving up your phone book?" Lance asked.

"'Cause I'm going to be in a one-on-one quality relationship," I announced.

"Who's the victim?" Connie chuckled.

"Does this have anything to do with Doug's wedding?" Jenks inquired. He was also known as "Doc," but we used "Jenks," as did a lot of his cohorts, to cut down on confusion with my roommate, Joseph "Doc" Holliday.

"You guessed it, Jenks," Doc said.

"Her name is Honore, and *I'm* the 'victim'—a willing victim," I responded. "And it's not about Doug getting married. It's about me getting tired of running the streets."

"Watch out, y'all," Big Dan said, "he might get hit by a bolt of lightning."

More laughter.

"Tired of the streets? Yeah, right!" Dab scoffed. "Now Honore *is* a bad chick, no doubt, but I can't see you giving up on the streets. No way. Not you."

"Now, I have to agree with Dab on that," Trace spoke up. "Doug was different; you could see that his heart wasn't in it anymore when it came to chasing these skirts. But you, Davey? C'mon, man; we've all been knowing you for a long, long time. Chasing skirts is what you're good at! But if you're serious, I'll take that black book!"

"I'll take it too," Big Dan said.

"Me three." Rich chuckled.

"Me four," added Guy.

"I don't know why folks think I *have to* chase women," I began.

"Not 'have to,'" Dab corrected. "*Want* to."

"It's in your blood-ski," added Doc.

"It's the dawg in you." Big Dan laughed.

Just then four cuties came in and sat at a table not far from ours. Two of them were superstars; the other two were just stars.

Damn! I thought as I watched them.

"Look at you," Connie commented. "You got the scent already. I can see your nostrils flaring."

Everyone cracked up.

"Naw, naw, naw," I lied, "I, uh … I thought I, uh … knew one of them."

"You mean you *want* to know one of them," amended Dab. "Admit it, man; you ain't ready for no one-on-one relationship yet."

"Davey, look," Lance said, "we all go through that stage when we think we're ready; I know I did. But you got to be honest with yourself—"

"Look who's talking," interrupted Jenks, laughing. Lance had ladies living in three different houses that he owned.

"The day *will* come when it'll be true," continued Lance, "but don't select the day; let the day select you."

Connie laughed. "Damn, that's good advice from one dog to another."

"Hey, Honore's a bad babe, man," Rich chipped in. "Don't fuck her up."

"No, just fuck her down." Connie chuckled.

"C'mon, guys," Guy said, "listen to Davey. He's a grown man like the rest of us. He should know when it's time for him to settle down."

"You mean he's a grown *dog*," joked Connie.

"We're not saying that he don't know," Jenks submitted, "but those four ladies walking in just now shows that he has to tighten up if he thinks the time is now."

"Yeah, if he was out with Honore and she saw him look at another cutie," Rich said, "that'd be the end of that one-on-one."

"See? I don't do that when I'm out with a lady," informed I.

"That's not what my cousin Bertha said," Doc tendered.

"Well, if I did it when I was out with Bertha," I offered, "it must have been when she had that false makeup on."

"Wrong-ski!" Doc corrected. "When she was wearing that makeup, you never took her out anywhere. Remember?"

"Okay, okay," I said to the group, "The bottom line is this. From yesterday on, I'm involved in a one-on-one. It has nothing to do with

Doug getting married. It has nothing to do with lack of prospects. It has nothing to do with what y'all think. It's just about me doing the right thing for me. And I think Honore is the right thing."

"More power to you, buddy-ski," Doc congratulated.

"Do your thing, man," Dab said, "but I'm gonna have my I-told-you-so speech ready."

Everyone laughed.

"You ain't gon' have a reason to say it," I predicted. *Damn, that girl at that table is looking good!*

The weeks went by.

Aura did come to Rendezvous that following Friday, and she was looking better than good—good enough to eat. And I mean that literally. But I didn't even ask her for her phone number. I was on good behavior. No more girl-chasing. I'd even trashed my black books. I had put them in a trash bag in the can in my room.

Honore had my heart, I felt. She told me that Chauncey had called her a couple of times trying to explain, but she didn't want to hear it. She told him that she wasn't interested and that she had her man back.

And back I was. We did everything together: went to movies, plays, picnics at the beaches in Malibu, and out to dinner at least once a week. She cooked for me, I cooked for her, and we had Blockbuster weekends.

I was spending the majority of the time at her place. She suggested that I move in with her, but I told her that I would probably start looking for a place of my own soon. She liked that too but suggested that I just stay with her until I found a spot. I think she just wanted me out of the Mini-Mansion and away from the fellas.

Her girlfriends were behind that, more than likely. She would hang with them on Friday nights when I was at Rendezvous, but they would not go there. The club was my space, she resolved, but she requested that I call her just before we closed each Friday night to see whether she wanted me to come over. She usually did. That request bothered me a little, but I brushed the thought aside. I did like seeing her after the club closed.

Aura started coming to the club every Friday with a girlfriend or two. I refrained from hitting on her, as fine as she was. But we did talk when she came through. We became friends. I even told her about Honore and what a great woman she was. She said that she was happy for me. She always came to the club early and would leave about eleven because of her babysitter.

Then, one Friday, about five weeks into my relationship with Honore, Aura came to the club alone. She got there after ten, and at eleven o'clock she was still there. I saw her come up the stairs to the VIP room as I was talking to Dab, Jenks, Guy, and Big Dan. We were standing at the thick glass wall overlooking the dance floor below, drinking champagne, and checking out the CODs. She went to the bar.

"Damn!" Jenks exclaimed when he saw Aura. "Who is *that*?" Whenever he came to the club, he'd buy bottles of the bubbly to share with us, which caused him to coin a nickname for the pinochle crew: "the Bubbling Brothas."

"A friend," I said,

"Uh huh," Big Dan said with a smirk.

I went over to the bar as she was ordering a piña colada.

"You're still here?" I asked, looking at my watch.

She smiled when she saw me. "Yes. Randolph is out of town with his father for the rest of the summer, so no more babysitter for a while. Hallelujah."

I laughed. "So where are your girls tonight?"

"They had other plans," she said. "I decided to come alone, thinking that maybe you'd look out for me."

"No problem," I consented. "I got your back."

"Just my back?"

"I got your front too." I chuckled. "I got your whole body."

She smiled. "Mmm hmm."

"Let me introduce you to some folks." I led her over to the fellas. After a while, she was laughing, joking, and drinking champagne with the crew as if they were old friends. Dab and I took turns leaving and interacting with our partners to make sure the club was running smoothly. A few other ladies ventured over to the assemblage. Doc, Rich, Denn, and a couple of the other partners, Stew and Ronaldo, came upstairs, and our little group took over the VIP room until closing.

After last call was announced, we tried to decide on whether to go to Jerry's Deli, Kate Mantilini, the Beverly Hills café, or Berrie's for something to eat. Aura pulled me aside.

"Uh, Davey," she began, "I think I might have had one champagne too many. Do you mind if I ride with you to get something to eat?"

"I told you I had your back, right?" I reminded.

"Yes, you did." She interlocked her arm with mine.

"We decided on Kate Mantilini," Dab told me.

"Cool," I responded. "We'll meet you guys over there."

After I paid the valet for Aura's car, telling them that we were going to leave it there in the lot behind the club, I drove down LaCienega toward Wilshire, trying not to look at her creamy thighs as she sat with crossed legs in my passenger seat. We were coming up on Fatburger on the left.

"I can't believe it's not crowded over there yet," she commented.

"It'll be crowded in a few minutes," I assured her.

"I know that's right," she agreed, and then she hesitated. "Uh, you know ..."

I read her mind. "You want one, huh?"

Her eyes lit up. "Do you?"

"Who told you."

I made a U-turn past San Vicente and doubled back to the hamburger joint. I parked on the side street behind the little restaurant, got her order, and went to the window. We decided to eat there in the car when I brought back her burger and my Kingburger. She had coffee with hazelnut cream with hers. I had red pop. We sat there and talked and ate.

"You know, your friends are marveling about you and your relationship with your girl," she shared as we were eating. "They said that they've never seen you that into a woman before."

"Yeah, well I'm amazed too," I admitted.

"That's very commendable." She smiled. "And also attractive in a man."

"But tell me this," I asked. "Why do women think they have to put pressure on a guy when things are going good?"

"What kind of pressure?"

"Wanting me to move out of the house I'm living in with the fellas and move in with her, wanting me to call her before I leave the club to see if she wants me to come by or not every Friday."

"She's doing that?"

"Yep."

"Did you call her tonight?"

"Nope. I'm rebelling." I laughed.

"Well, from what you told me about the house you live in, the Mini-Mansion, I guess she's afraid of the temptations that may come your way."

"You're the biggest temptation that has come my way lately."

"Really?"

"And I haven't bothered you, right?"

"Right. I just figured that I wasn't your type."

"Are you kidding me? You are *definitely* my type. If you looked up 'Davey's type' in the dictionary, you'd see your picture."

She laughed.

"Well, I didn't know what to think. After all these weeks, you've never made a pass at me since our initial meeting in the park. You haven't even asked for my phone number."

"I wanted to, but I felt that I wouldn't be able to resist calling you. I can only stand so much temptation." I chuckled.

"That's why it's commendable what you're doing. You're successfully resisting a woman who's turned on by you." She was looking directly in my eyes now.

I returned her look, setting my half-eaten burger on the console between us, next to hers. I leaned in, as did she. Her hazel eyes were mesmerizing.

What am I doing? I chided myself as our lips crept closer together. *I have Honore! I have the one-on-one relationship I craved!*

I'm not supposed to be interested in another! I'm not supposed to desire another! I'm definitely not supposed to be kissing another!

I kissed another. I passionately kissed another. Our tongues parried. I surrounded hers with my lips and gently sucked it as she caressed my face with her soft hand. I caressed her back and butt with my hard hand.

And that wasn't the only thing that was hard. We kissed even deeper.

Our eyes opened simultaneously.

"Do you want to follow me home?" she asked softly.

"Who told you."

I took her back to her car and followed her to her condo. I was mildly surprised that she also lived in Fox Hills. *I should have figured that she lived in or near there, since she was jogging in the park,* I thought. In fact, she lived around the corner from Honore.

Honore. Should I call her? I pondered. *And why am I feeling guilty?*

The guilty feeling stayed with me for the hour and a half that I spent at Aura's. Yeah, an hour and a half! That's all the time I needed. We never left her couch.

After some heavy petting and kissing, I worked her thong off and had an after-midnight snack. She returned the favor with me leaning back on her sofa. A very talented mouth she had. It didn't take me long to succumb.

She tried to lead me into her bedroom when she was done, but my indiscretion was overwhelming. I told her I had to go. We kissed at the door, and then she let me leave. This time I took her phone number.

I called Honore from the phone booth on the corner and told her I was on the way and would be there in a few minutes. Sleepily, she acquiesced. I let myself in with my key that she'd insisted I take so I wouldn't have to wait for her at the door in case she was knocked out.

"Hi, baby," she greeted when I entered the bedroom. "How was the club?"

"Crowded," I answered, yawning.

"Why didn't you call me before you left there?" She watched me getting undressed.

"We were debating on where to go for breakfast. I got caught up."

"Who all went?"

"Doc, Dab, Jenks, Denn, Big Dan, Guy, Rich ..."

"No females?"

"The fellas invited a few. I can't remember their names." I got under the covers with her warm body. She was entirely naked. I felt myself getting aroused. It poked her.

"What's this I feel?" She smiled. And before I could answer, she pushed back the covers and sniffed my penis.

What the! I thought as I lay there. *I'm glad I didn't wash my dick as I was washing my face and hands before I left Aura's. If Honore smelled a just-washed penis, she would definitely be suspicious. But she smelled it! She smelled my dick! That's a first. This lady is more insecure than I would've guessed. Do I want to be involved with a lady that will go to that extreme to see if I've been messing around? What would she do if she knew I'd been with another, even though I didn't go all the way?*

She had a puzzled look on her face when she laid her head on my chest, pulling the sheet and comforter up to cover us.

"I'm tired, baby," she said. Five minutes later, she was sound asleep.

I lay there thinking about Aura, and I wondered why I had felt guilty when I was at her place but now was wishing I had stayed there a little longer and had gone all the way. And I realized that it was not because Aura was a beautiful, sexy, voluptuous woman. It was because Aura was *another* woman, a *different* woman.

I still craved variety! I was fighting the hemmed-in feeling.

So what am I doing with Honore's keys? I asked myself before sleep came.

The acrid smell of something burning drifted past my nose and woke me up. I looked around in a panic. That's when I saw the dying smoking embers in an ashtray on the nightstand by my head.

It was the charred remains of the paper that Aura had written her number on.

What the fuck? I thought. I heard Honore in the kitchen. The smell of bacon overpowered the burning scent.

Now I gotta go in here and deal with this?

I lay there for a while, deciding how to handle this situation. After pulling on my pants, I got out of bed and headed to the kitchen, deciding not to say anything about the phone number unless she did. Hell, it had been an easy number anyway. I had it memorized.

Honore was looking sexy in her pink baby doll as she placed some bread in the toaster. While she waited for it to pop up, she poured some coffee in her cup and added some creamer. I walked up behind her and wrapped my arms around her small waist. She pushed her butt back at me as she tasted her coffee.

"Debra will be here in a half hour," she said between sips. "We're going shopping."

"And why not?" I joked. "It's Saturday, ain't it?"

"Very funny. So are you going to stay here or go home?"

"Home, James."

"You're so corny." Honore chuckled. "That's one of the things I like about you."

What are the things you don't like?

I kissed the back of her neck as I rubbed the back of her lower body with the front of my lower body.

"Don't start nothing that we don't have time to finish," she warned. Then I saw her forehead wrinkle, as she sniffed her coffee. "Hmm, that's what it was."

"What?"

"I smelled something that reminded me of this hazelnut creamer on you last night."

I thought about her sniffing Junior. And I remembered the coffee that Aura drank at Fatburger before she used her mouth on me.

"I've never had anyone do that to me before," I said to the back of her head.

"Shante and Debra said that we can catch you guys off guard like that." She laughed. "If it smells funky, we'll know what you've been doing. If it smells just washed, again, we'll know what you've been doing. I don't know what smelling something like hazelnut means."

"Well, a man does touch many things with his hands, and he uses those selfsame hands to touch something else when he goes to the bathroom. I mean, I wash my hands before I leave the bathroom, not *before* I use it."

"I ain't sweating it." She turned to face me. "Why are you?"

"I'm not sweating it either," I said quickly. "It was just strange to me."

"Uh, did you sleep good?"

"Uh, yeah," I answered, thinking about the ashtray.

"Well, let's eat so I can get ready to go."

Okay, I mused, *so she's not going to mention the phone number—yet. Hmm, I'd better be careful with this girl or just get while the getting's good. She's got some strange tendencies.*

After breakfast, I took a quick shower and left before Debra arrived. I thought about giving Aura a call when I got home but decided against it. I had some more soul-searching to do. When I reached the Mini-Mansion, I headed straight to the kitchen to grab a brewski out of the refrigerator. Doc was in there making a sandwich.

"The playa is home," he called out.

I heard Dab's door open upstairs and his footsteps coming down the stairs to the kitchen.

"Now, why do I have to be all that?" I asked as I retrieved a cold MGD.

"Man, I'm just kidding-ski," Doc assured me. "We know who you are. The question is, Do you?"

"Yeah," Dab said, entering the kitchen. "When you didn't show at Kate Mantilini's, I knew the deal. Can I use my I-told-you-so speech now?"

"Yeah, man, go 'head." I sighed. "Hmmph. I really thought I wanted to be in a one-on-one. But I guess the dog in me had other plans. I'm just not the one for a one-on-one—yet."

"Or maybe Honore is not *the* one-on-one-ski," suggested Doc.

"Amigos, we gotta be who we are," Dab philosophized. "And as long as we're not lying to these women, as long as we're not using the *L*-word loosely, as long as we're just enjoying life—just like they are—we ain't dogs."

"I know I'm not a dog," Doc quipped. "I'm just a puppy in training."

"Regardless of what women think," continued Dab, "none of us in this house are dogs. We're not using these ladies; we're not dogging them. We take them out, show them a good time; they enjoy our company, and we enjoy theirs. We satisfy them; they satisfy us."

"There's definitely no dogging in that," Doc agreed.

"You're right," I realized. "If I'm a dawg, I'm a friendly dawg. *Woman's* best friend kind of dawg. I'll protect her, I'm relatively reliable, and I'll lick her hand."

"Yeah." Doc chuckled. "And that's not all you'll lick."

"Now, there are men out there who *do* dog ladies," added Dab. "But that ain't us! We ain't got nothing to be ashamed of. We're dawgs, but we don't dog women. When our relationships are over, we're still friends with the ladies, and they're friends with us. Right?"

"Right-ski," Doc cosigned. "If you feel like you gotta dog a lady, you should end the relationship."

"Uh, fellas," I said, "some weird shit happened to me this morning."

"What?" Dan asked.

"First of all, I went home with Aura."

"Who told you," stated Dab sarcastically.

"Then, when I got to Honore's, she was half-asleep, but she smelled my dick when I got in bed with her."

"She did what-ski!" exclaimed Doc.

"Smelled my dick! And this morning when I woke up," I went on, "I saw Aura's phone number that she gave me last night burning in an ashtray by the bed."

"Whoa!" Doc yelled.

"That means she went through your pants pockets," deduced Dab.

"Who told you," I said *very* sarcastically.

"What did Honore say?" asked Doc.

"She didn't say shit," I replied. "She just fixed breakfast for us."

"And you *ate* it?" Doc asked.

"Man, you'd better leave that girl alone!" warned Dab.

"Yeah, she sounds like the kind of quiet girl that will really go off on a brothah," added Doc. "Go off big-ski! And I *know* you don't like drama."

"And it sounds like you're getting close to the dogging stage," Dab insinuated. "So it's like I said, you ain't ready to give up the chase, brothah. Don't fight it. If you gotta dog them, let 'em go."

Dab was right. I went up to my room with my beer, put on some jazz, and lay on top of the covers, thinking.

During the weeks that I was reinvolved with Honore, I still got calls from other women that I knew, and I still saw ladies out and at the club that looked good to me, but I fought the urge to attempt to get with them. However, I realized that I *did* have the urges. I didn't want to have any urges to be with another. I wanted a lady that would stop me from having the urges, not one that would just stop me from acting on them.

The lady I want would have me without really trying. It would just be natural—second nature. For some of us guys, it takes time to run across a lady like that—a lady that will *make* you not want to be with another, without even trying. I could tell that Doug had that with Copper. We were all on different clocks. I realized that no matter how badly I wanted it to happen, I could not rush the process.

Some of us take a little longer to get serious. Some of us have so much fun having fun that the years slip by in bunches and we suddenly realize that it ain't that much fun anymore.

Or in the midst of having fun, a special lady appears and you realize that being with her is even more fun; it's all you want to do.

That's when you *know* you've met the one.

Eventually, I will be ready to settle down with that special woman, but that day hasn't come yet. Doug got married because he met Copper, his soul mate. He didn't search for her. She just happened to walk into his life while he was enjoying life.

My way of enjoying life means working at my employment agency and Rendezvous, having events at the house, chasing women, and hanging with the fellas. Somehow my mate—the one—is going to have to just wiggle and sneak in there. She's going to have to find her own way in. I won't fight her when she comes, but I will not force the issue either. I'm sure I'll recognize her. I'll recognize the feeling. It won't be contrived. And then my "friendly dog" days will happily be over.

I heard the doorbell ring.

"Davey-ski!" Doc called out.

I went to my door and saw Honore coming up the stairs. She was looking good as hell, but she had an apologetic look on her face.

"Hey you," I greeted as she reached me.

"I'm sorry for dropping by without calling," she apologized as I motioned her into my room and shut the door, "but something was bothering me while I was out with Debra."

Yeah, well, something was bothering me too, I thought.

"Have a seat." I indicated the bed, but she sat in one of my cushioned chairs by the window.

"Davey, I don't think it's gonna work," she blurted out. "You are a very nice guy in your own way, but I still don't think you're ready yet. You're not ready for a one-on-one. I mean, you came to me last night with a phone number in your pocket!"

"Baby." I sighed. "I think I'm gonna have to agree with you. *You* are the best thing that has happened to me, and yet I find my eyes and mind still wandering. I'm beginning to think that there's something wrong with *me*."

"There's nothing wrong with you, Davey," she declared. "You're just a man."

"What does that mean? Being a man means I can't have a one-on-one? That I can't be happy in a relationship? That I have to cheat?"

"No, no, and no," she answered. "It doesn't mean that. It means that *you* have to make up *your* mind what you *really* want in life— what's *really* important to *you*. And *you* have to act on it with determination, with integrity, with your whole heart involved."

"Yeah, I thought that's what I was doing," I muttered.

"Are you sure that's what you thought? Or was loneliness or wanting to be like your friend, Doug, playing a part?"

"I know I don't want to be a bachelor for life," I affirmed.

"And I don't want to be a bachelorette." She laughed. "*But* neither of us should settle."

"You think I was settling with you? You were settling with me?"

"No," she said, "I really wanted you. I wasn't settling, but I want to be really wanted too. So now I want to step back, regroup, and let you step back and regroup too. We can stay friends. Hell, I might even entertain some creeping with you, but I want you to do your thing, and I'll do mine, and we'll see where the chips may fall. If we're meant to be, we will be; if not, we'll be happy with whatever or whoever comes."

She stood up. I went to her and we hugged tightly and warmly. I wanted to kiss her, but I held back. What she had proposed was right on target, and I wanted to let it marinate.

After she left, I lay on the bed, contemplating our conversation. I was thinking about the future, thinking about the possibilities, and thinking about Aura's phone number.

Suddenly I jumped up as a thought hit me. *The maid came Thursday!* My little black books were in my trash can!

They were irreplaceable. They contained my past and possibly my future. I darted to the trash bag in the black trash bin. It was empty. I rushed into the bathroom. I was sweating now. Again I found an empty bag.

I started cursing Bebe, the maid, as I rushed down the stairs, past Doc and Dab, and out the kitchen door to the two big trash cans by the garage. One was empty, and the other was half-full. The fellas were standing at the kitchen door, looking at me.

Just as I made up my mind to start digging through the garbage in the one can, I heard Dab and Doc laughing.

"It ain't funny, man," I said. "I put my phone books in the trash, but I wasn't going to throw them away."

"Oh really?" Doc asked. "Doesn't putting something in the trash mean you're getting *rid* of it?"

"I was contemplating it," I said. "My mind wasn't made up yet. I didn't need *your* girl to make my mind up for me! *Yo'* girl threw my shit away!"

"Three things," Dab replied, still chuckling. "First of all, she ain't my girl. She's my *ex*-girl. Second, *you* threw your shit away. In the trash *is* away. *But,* third, she *didn't.* She saw your phone books in the trash and gave them to me to hold for you. She said she had a feeling you'd be looking for them someday."

"Whew!" I exclaimed as I headed back inside the house. "She did that? Bebe is all right with me. Give her a kiss for me."

"You give her a kiss for you," Dab suggested. "She might like that. Hell, *you* might like that."

He and Doc laughed.

"Naw, I wouldn't like it," I corrected. "She's your girl, your ex. For me to do that, I'd really be a *dog.* Not me. Me? I'm just a guy in his thirties who is not gon' keep denying who I am. I like women, but I want one to *love.* However, I can't rush it. God will let me know when the time is right. *He'll* let me know when she's ready for me to find her. Until then, I'm just gon' be happy and enjoy my life."

"Yep, know who you are, Davey-ski," added Doc, still laughing. "You can't help yo' self. You just gots to chase da cat. It's nuttin' but the *dawg* in you."

Maybe for now, I thought. *For now, but not that much longer. She's out there ... somewhere.*

Printed in the United States
By Bookmasters